ONE FAT ENGLISHMAN

ONE FAT ENGLISHMAN

by

KINGSLEY AMIS

HARCOURT, BRACE & WORLD, INC.
NEW YORK

To
JANE

first American edition 1964
Library of Congress Catalog Card Number: 64-11532
Printed in the United States of America

CHAPTER I

'WHAT'S HE LIKE?'

'Oh, you'll find him pleasant enough, I should imagine. Very ready to laugh. Not much sense of humour, though. He's a bit fiercely Danish.'

'You mean that's why he doesn't have much sense of humour? Because of this being fiercely Danish?'

'Not necessarily, but no doubt there's some connection. The Scandinavians are dear people but they've never been what you might call bywords for wit and sparkle, have they? Any more than the Germans. Still, what I really meant was, he's apt to get sort of extra Danish when his wife's about. Which is most of the time. I suppose he feels he has to work at the Danish thing. You see, she thinks she's American, but according to him she's Danish.'

'Which of them is right?'

'Well, in a way they both are. Legally she is. She was born in Denmark and her parents brought her over here when she was about ten. They settled down in Idaho or Iowa or somewhere. Then when she was twenty-one or -two she went back on a visit and met Ernst and stayed on and married him. That was just about the time he was starting his job on what you would call the faculty at the university in Copenhagen. Then he got sabbatical leave and got a year's appointment at Budweiser and of course brought Helene and the kid with him. So she's an American citizen who's spent well over half her life in another country, the one she was born in. It's a curious—'

'Does it matter which she is, Danish or American?'

'Oh, I think so, don't you? Don't you think that sort of thing always matters terribly? Anyway, it certainly does in this case. She wants them to stay on over here, he says. He wants them to go back to Copenhagen when he finishes at Budweiser next summer. If not before. He doesn't like it much.'

'At Budweiser?'

'Over here in general. He finds himself strongly—'

'How long has he been in the United States?'

'Six weeks, about, but—'

'First trip?'

'Yes, but you must try to remember, Joe, that these days people know really quite a bit about America before they ever arrive here, what with films and television shows and these little things who sing and even the odd *book* I suppose you'd have to say, and visiting Americans and all the—'

'Know? Quite a bit? How true a picture do you think is given by this kind of stuff?'

'Well...it's an introduction, anyway.'

'Would you like some more in there?'

'Thank you, just a small one.'

The man who had been asking all the questions, a tall thinnish American of fifty called Joe Derlanger, moved some yards off. The man who had been giving all the answers, a shortish fat Englishman of forty called Roger Micheldene, sat and thought for a moment. Then he removed his tan-and-slate tweed jacket.

Even in the shade of the trees by the swimming-pool it was very hot, much hotter than it had any right to be in the last week in October. Sweat crawled and tickled among the thin wisps of red hair on the crown of his head. There was a small trough of it in the fold behind each knee. He creaked with it whenever he moved. He would have liked to take off far more than his jacket, but knew he was the wrong shape for this. For instance, his mammary development would have been acceptable only if he could have shed half his weight as well as changing his sex. The lateral fusion of his waist and hips made the wearing of braces necessary. After more thought he removed these too and stuffed them into a pocket. A couple of inches broad, scarlet with royal-blue silhouettes of fish, they had gone down rather satisfactorily at home, but over here might seem no more than affected.

Although he normally made a point of not conforming to American usage or taste in the smallest particular, Roger did not want to look affected today. He did not want to look fat either, but all he could do about that was to stay as fully clothed as was consistent with not dying of heatstroke. He opened the top few buttons of his shirt, peeled it from his chest, blew several times into the aperture, and rebuttoned.

Joe Derlanger came back from the place by the changing-huts where the outdoor drinks were kept, carrying two huge gin and tonics. He wore a yellow towelling shirt over what Roger saw as a pair of elongated bathing shorts with a pattern reminiscent of cushion-covers in typists' flats. On his feet were what Roger had heard called sneakers. Apart from the natural endowment of thick blue-grey hairs on forearms and calves, he wore nothing else that was visible. He looked a good twenty degrees cooler than Roger felt. Good luck to him, Roger thought to himself. Or fairly good luck to him. If being cool meant dressing like a child there was a clear case for staying hot.

Joe handed Roger his drink with a glance of intimate grimness, like a gang-leader dealing out small arms before a job. 'What does he do exactly, this Ernst Bang? Bang? Is that really a guy's name? What does he do, anyhow?'

'It's quite a common name in some parts of Scandinavia. He's a philologist. Germanic, naturally.'

'Philologist. That's words and syllables, isn't it?'

'That kind of thing. Ernst is something of an authority on the North Germanic languages, especially Early Icelandic and Faroese.'

'Sounds compelling, doesn't it? But what do they want with an Early Icelandic buff at a place like . . .? Wait a minute.'

He had turned in his chair, looking over towards the point, a hundred yards away, where a track left the metalled road to curve round in front of the house. Here a large green-and-brown car was moving. It began to raise a cloud of dust.

'This must be them now.' Joe got up and faced the house, fifty yards away in a different direction. He called in a voice of great volume and harshness of tone: 'Grace. Grace, they're here.'

'All right,' the reply came in a voice of at least equal power and only about a major third up the scale.

'Well, come on down.'

'All right.'

With a shrug and a jerk of the head, Joe moved to the nearby shelter and pulled more chairs out of it, arranging them round the concrete walk by the pool. He did this in the manner of a sadistic animal trainer. If anything looked like starting to go wrong for an instant there would be an outbreak of violence. This policy, Roger had noticed, marked all Joe's dealings with the world of objects.

Of the seven deadly sins, Roger considered himself qualified in gluttony, sloth and lust but distinguished in anger. The first time the two men met, an incident with a brief-case lock had suggested to him that here was a formidable rival in the last-named field. Only that morning Roger had gone into the bathroom to find all the towels very tightly tied by their corners to the chromium rail. The knots appeared to have been consolidated with water. He had wondered why this was until his own towel had twice fallen to the floor from the smooth metal. Joe seemed not to include people in his programme. He was one down on Roger there.

'I meant to tell you about this boy Irving Macher,' Joe said as he strove with the chairs. 'Brilliant young Jewish kid from New York. They don't come any smarter than that. In his junior year at Budweiser. On the staff of the *Lit.* there and already—'

'Junior year? Is that what you call the first year?'

'No, it's what we call the last year but one. And this novel of his. It is honestly the most sizzling thing you ever saw. It just about turns your insides over. It's about—'

'You mentioned it last night.'

'Oh, did I? Well, you can have a look at it tomorrow. We're all just wild about it. Hoping to rush it through for April.'

'What advance are you paying?'

'Two thousand, maybe two-five.'

'That's a lot for a first novel.'

'Ah, shows we believe in the goddam thing. You'll be able to take it, won't you, Rog?'

'Well, the last few American firsts we've done haven't gone down at all well, I'm sorry to say. There's a definite feeling against them on the Board at the moment.'

'This is something really exceptional.'

Talking and watching the car, which was now pulling up near the house, had told on Joe's vigilance with the chairs. The last of the bunch tried to lurch away from him towards the pool. He brought it back with a sharp twist of its arm, following this up with a kneeing in the behind. It squealed across the concrete on its iron toes.

Roger watched coldly, but felt his heart beating. 'I'm looking forward to seeing it,' he said.

'For Christ's sake where is that woman?' Joe asked

himself aloud. Then, using his whole tall body to wave, he shouted : 'Hallo. Come on over here. Down here.'

Five people approached over the gravel of the driveway and the clipped green grass. Three of them, two men and a woman, were unknown to Roger. Of the remaining two, who were talking animatedly to each other, one was Dr. Ernst Bang, Otto Jespersen Reader in Language Studies at the University of Copenhagen and currently Visiting Fellow at Budweiser College. The other was Roger's reason for being here now.

He got to his feet in good time and drew in his stomach, which had earlier started feeling tight, an impressive achievement for such a stomach. Memories ran in his brain. They were displaced by present longing when he took in his reason's variegated fair hair shining in the sun, face with thin but prominent mouth, rather topheavy body in a white dress with small blue and green things on it, long bare brown legs. Sixteen days to decide it one way or the other, he thought.

There were greetings and introductions. Roger relegated for later inspection, if that, the young man called Nigel Pargeter whose sole right to have turned up seemed to be that he was English. An American girl of college age, whose name Roger missed, deserved instant inspection, if nothing more. She was dark and looked foreign, though not in the usual sense of never smiling. She moved her hips and shoulders about a lot, too. But she was very clearly the property of Irving Macher.

Roger always remembered how quickly and completely he hated the author of *Blinkie Heaven*. Long afterwards it occurred to him that he had felt exactly the same excited repulsion on meeting a television producer, also American, at the Mirabelle. The chap had monopolised throughout the evening the attention of the fashionable Jesuit whom Roger had set out to impress and whose dinner he was paying for out of his own pocket : £5 10s. on wines alone. It was easy to underrate Mother Nature's early warning systems.

Brown-haired and freckled, with a mild crew-cut and a light-weight get-up of blue shirt and drill trousers, Irving Macher had nothing noticeable about him but a pair of restless grey eyes. Their restlessness indicated that there was nothing much for them to see rather than that they could not take in what they saw. This air of having found out a great deal by the age of twenty-one focused Roger's hatred. He would do something about Macher's air.

For the moment there were more important things on hand. Roger had last seen Dr. Bang three days earlier and fifteen miles away. With Mrs. Bang the figures were eighteen months and getting on for four thousand miles. And yet it was Dr. Bang who laughed and shook Roger's hand for ten seconds and grasped his shoulder and told him how good it was to see him. Mrs. Bang smiled slightly and gave Roger her cheek, or rather her jaw, to kiss in the way she had. He searched her manner for circumspect self-restraint, but could find none. Had it really been she, and not her husband, who had been away in Idaho or Iowa with the small Bang when he made his (unforewarned) descent on their house just off Budweiser campus? Yes, it really had.

'How are you, Helene? You're looking frightfully well.'

'Yes, I'm fine, thank you. What a lovely place this is and how kind of Mr. and Mrs. Derlanger to invite us over.'

'Oh, they always make a great thing of entertaining... You like it at Budweiser, I gather? They found you a reasonable house, anyway.'

'Yes, and the neighbours are fun, they're so kind, they're always in and out, and all the kids... I think the one who has most of a ball is Arthur.'

At the sound of this name Roger stiffened, a reaction fated to pass unnoticed in one of his figure. He also crossed himself mentally. He had always thought it malignly significant that every other Arthur he had met or heard of was well over thirty. Even at five years old there had been a dreadful maturity in Arthur Bang's regard, in the deliberate way he turned his head and seemed to reflect before he spoke. What must he be like now, rising seven? 'Oh yes, how is Arthur?' Roger asked solicitously.

'Just fine. He goes to this little farm school place where a lot of the faculty kids go, and the teachers are most impressed with him, especially his study habits and aptitudes.'

'Splendid, splendid.' This was an understatement. Without wanting to, Roger recalled trying to make verbal love to Helene in Regent's Park with Arthur looking up at him appraisingly from his push-chair, trying to hold her hand in the small room at Oskar Davidsen's while Arthur spat no. 91 (fried forcemeat cakes with red cabbage, meat jelly and beetroot) at him. School. Of course. It had had to come. Roger felt the emotions of a traditional French lover whose mistress's husband's reserve class is recalled.

'He's growing so fast. He was just a baby when you last saw him, wasn't he?'

'When I first saw him he was.' And no mean performer even then, the little bastard, inverting over the knee of Roger's new suit a whole dish of his grandma's home-made quince preserve, sent all the way from Idaho or Iowa for the purpose.

'Well, it must be three or four years since we met, mustn't it?'

'It was April 1961 in London,' Roger said, doing his best to dispel shock and disappointment from his voice.

Dr. Bang rarely stayed out of any conversation as long as this. Now he said in his uvular Danish tones: 'These women have no sense of time, have they, Roger? Oh yes, of course, we know, all of us, they've got other much more—'

'Oh yes we do have a sense of time, it's just that you didn't get around to appreciating it yet.'

'You hear that? Isn't it monstrous? There's nothing I can do about it, it seems. Try as I may, she's incorrigible. *Do have*—it's like something in Pope. And always the aorist tense instead of the perfect. She gets more American-ised every day, and of course the speech is where it first shows.'

'Come on,' Roger said, smiling, 'you're not on duty now. Let's have a drink.'

'I'm sorry, I can never learn better. As long as people are speaking round me, my job's never over. It's such a basic human activity, you can't keep away from it.'

'Well, I can think of one or two—'

'But look,' Helene said to her husband, 'from everything you told me about this I still can't figure out why it's so wrong to speak in the American way. More people speak like this than speak in the British way, after all.'

'But it's not the only—'

'There you are, Roger. Inability to conduct a logical discussion.' Ernst turned away and settled down to argue with Helene. 'It's not a question of right and wrong at all. Ideas of correctness don't enter in. Any more than the number of speakers. It's simply that in the Eastern Hemi-sphere, which as you know includes Scandinavia, the tradi-tional form of English, learnt as a second language, has been British English. Now—'

'But we aren't in the Eastern Hemisphere any more, we're in America, and it's just as traditional to—'

'It's not a question of traditional or not traditional, it's which particular—'

'You told me yourself you should never—'

Roger stayed close when, under Joe's direction, they went and sat down by the pool. Nearly half the time he spent in their company was regularly filled by the Bangs talking to each other. He was glad that for the moment they were talking English, which they tended to abandon for Danish when they got excited. Although he liked seeing what talking Danish did to Helene's mouth, the main effect was to make him feel excluded in some way.

The relatively close inspection of her he could now safely make showed that, at twenty-nine, she was looking better than ever, a slim girl with an endearingly dispro-portionate bosom. The slender hips, as far as could be seen, were still slender. So were the shoulders, with a couple of millimetres more flesh over the collarbones that showed through the lightly tanned skin. Then, as a face-fetichist of many years' standing, Roger shifted his glance upwards.

That was where the best (by a narrow margin) of her was. With that thin mouth and that thin nose and those heavy eyes she had a look of unawakened brutality that went straight to more than one part of his frame. Then there was that hair. Its range of colour, from ash through pale gold to lemon, was perhaps excessive, coming close to offending his sense of the fitness of things. As always, it was slightly tousled. And, as often, her cheeks were slightly flushed. When he first saw her, walking over to join his party in the Langeliniepavillonen five years earlier, he had seriously thought she might have come straight from a hurried passage with the doorman or even the hat-and-coat girl. By the end of the evening he had had to conclude that this could not have been. Pity, actually, if one took a long enough view.

What, at any rate, did she see in Dr. Bang? Or rather (Christ) find, like, seem to think she wanted to stick to? For visually Dr. Bang had plenty to offer, what with his

height and youth and *slimness* and small delicate dark
head, all the appearance of a ballet dancer gifted with unusually expressive powers of mime. (Not much more than
ten years ago Roger might have considered taking on the
good Doctor himself. But he had finished with all that
now.) Orally, or aurally, the husband of Helene had less
to offer. Then why was she always talking to him? True,
they were usually arguing, but this denoted interest on her
part. And how could she have that?

Both Bangs, after a vehement couple of sentences in
Danish, now turned on Roger. They talked to him simul-
taneously, a thing they often did when not talking to each
other. Roger tried to divide his attention fairly, being very
cordial. People like him had to take every chance they got
of being that.

'All this opposition, it's enough to make a man—'

'—thing you're going to give up in a hurry. Why, some
women would give their eye-teeth to—'

'—putting any pressure on her at all. It's a question of
the normal—'

'—born over there and of course I speak the language,
but it says on my passport that I'm a—'

'—to do is make formal application to the authorities,
which in the case of a Danish—'

'—stay that way.'

'—more or less automatically.'

Roger took advantage of the joint lull to be the voice of
reason and moderation, two things which, as with cordial-
ity, he had to keep a sharp look-out for opportunities of
being the voice of. It was the easier because the Bangs had
had this argument before, every time he had met them, in
fact, though usually later in the day. No doubt being in
America encouraged it.

Taking a pinch of Town Clerk from his pewter snuff-
box, Roger said: 'I can quite see Helene's position, Ernst.

The fact that she wants to hang on to her American citizenship doesn't mean she feels in the least unhappy or in any way disloyal or—'

'Exactly, that's what I keep—'

'—you or Denmark. On the other hand, Helene, you must realise that the custom is for a wife to take her husband's nationality, and since Denmark is your—'

'If you could only get her to—'

'—seem natural that you should make this application one of these days.'

Roger disliked taking Ernst's part against Helene, but in this matter the more people who did so the better, from his point of view. A fully Danish Helene seemed more likely to stay in Denmark, which was handy for England. A persistently American Helene somehow brought up the fact that there were more Americans than Danes, and than British too for that matter. And, also somehow, not only more of them either.

'When you've got back home, Helene,' Roger went on, exploiting the weightiness that was weight's only dividend, 'you'll—'

'But this country is my home,' Helene broke in at full stretch : 'that's what I've been trying to—'

'She and I were born in the same—'

'—here, but he's the most obstinate—'

'—drink, or would you like to take a swim while the sun lasts?'

Joe's abrasive tones, or possibly his subject-matter, halted them. Dr. Bang's consort shaded her eyes and looked up at Joe with an easy grace, and a display of lifted breast, and ditto of armpit, that half-filled Roger with fury. He had had to get used to the idea that three was company, but he was clear in his mind that four was not.

'Why, I'd just love to,' Helene said, with a smile that

showed off her world-class square white teeth, 'but I'm afraid I don't have a swimsuit.'

'I haven't got a costume either,' Ernst said.

'Oh, no problem, hell, plenty of spares in the changing-huts. You never can tell who might be turning up, you know. Forethought. That's the thing. If you'd like to come along with me, Dr. Bang—'

'Ernst, please.'

'Ernst, and my wife will take care of you, Mrs. Bang—'

'Helene.' For once, there was a good deal of Danishness in the way she spoke.

'Grace, find Helene something, will you, sweetheart? Fine. Now what about you, Rog, old man? You look as if you could do with a—'

'Thank you, Joe, no, I won't, if it's all the same to you.'

'Suit yourself.'

They all went away then.

CHAPTER II

Roger's decision not to swim had been among the easiest of his life. For a man as keen as he on getting into bed with women, keeping hidden the full enormity of his fatness was a chronic problem. Its most acute form naturally came up when someone new had to be hustled or cajoled past the point of no return. That point tended to get later and later as his belly waxed. The merest glimpse of it might be enough, even at a very advanced stage, to remind a girl of her obligations to family tradition, to husband or boy friend or host or room-mate or landlady, to humanity. But not only that. Recent experience suggested that that belly, exposed in a moment of inattention or abandon, could cause total withdrawal of favours previously granted. In other words, it tended to stop them. Cold. At any time.

This must not be allowed to happen with Helene. It was a crying shame that, temperamentally, she was different from his usual sort of girl. His usual sort of girl tended not to take it personally when he slept with them and this could lead to a lot of rather loose behaviour. Helene, on the other hand, was always very strict. In particular, she insisted on something like parity of nudity. She would not put on anything like a show for him while he sat about in faultless West of England tweeds. In the intervals of choking with rage and lust over this policy of hers, Roger saw it as not unreasonable. But it meant that the really detailed inspection of her which he longed to make would have to be paid for by giving her the chance of making a roughly equally really detailed inspection of him if she were so minded. So no go. So he had had to make do with a couple of glimpses of the side of her as she skipped out of or into bed, the back of her as she dressed or undressed, a small part of the top of the front of her before she switched out the light.

So seeing her in a bathing suit, he told himself without fear of contradiction, was going to be significant. He would be gaining visual experience of her body, if not neat, then in a higher concentration than he had had a chance of getting used to. He hoped it would not be too strong for him. With a slight smile of complacency at his own fore-thought, he reached into his jacket pocket for his sun-glasses and put them on. Provided he could remember to move his head about slightly from time to time, nobody would now be able to tell where he was looking. Any involuntary bulging of the eyeballs would likewise be masked. It occurred to him, as he watched carefully for Helene's reappearance, that he might throw away these advantages if he went on behaving like a seated figure carved out of old red sandstone. He shifted in his chair, mopped his face. took a pinch of snuff, attacked his drink, glanced about.

Only Grace Derlanger and, more surprisingly, Irving Macher had failed to go and change. They stood talking a few yards off. Or rather Macher was talking. He was doing it in a deep and rather resonant voice which Roger considered he had no right to. Any more than he had a right to a two- or two-and-a-half-thousand-dollar advance.

'And you're justified in acquiring money,' Macher was saying, as if in self-defence. 'More than that, it's your duty. We've gotten over all that other stuff now, that junk about it's your duty not to have money. Whoever did that duty? And duty's a thing people do, not something they don't do. Listen, what would you do to a soldier who went into a battle without taking his gun along? You'd have him

court-martialled, wouldn't you? And you'd be right. Somebody who can't protect himself weakens other people's
power of self-protection. Armies understand this. And a lot
more. An army's the right kind of organisation because it
only exists to do what's necessary. Nothing stuck on afterwards for the look of the thing. It's a pity nobody can use
them any more, armies. All we have now is scientists, and
they're no good. No good in the way I'm looking for. Too
much aesthetics about the whole idea.

'But going back to money: it's a terrific liberation to
think of it in the right way. My parents have money and I
like and admire them for it. It used to bother me a little,
knowing so much of it was around and hearing about it all
the time, but not any more. Money's good.'

Roger got the last part of this at close range, for Grace
Derlanger, seeing him sitting on his own, had walked her
companion over. She settled her stocky body efficiently in
a nearby chair, gazing at Macher through her thick glasses
but not moving a muscle of her face. It was hard to tell
whether or not she thought she was having nonsense talked
to her. Roger guessed she did, though without feeling as
much conviction as he would have liked. To be sure about
nonsense he had to be able to classify it, assign it to a
family tree of liberal nonsense, humanist-humanitarian nonsense, academic nonsense, Protestant nonsense, Freudian
nonsense and so on. Macher's nonsense stopped before he
could get deep enough into it.

Willingly turning his head, Roger saw that the Bangs
were approaching. Ernst had his arm round Helene's
shoulders, partly screening her from view, though not
enough to conceal the fact that her bathing suit was in two
widely separated pieces. With much loud chatter, Joe and
Pargeter, the Englishman, joined them by the diving-board,
closely followed by Macher's girl. The group was in continuous movement, so that Helene was only visible for

unpredictable instants. Roger sat watching like a sniper waiting for a clear shot at a general.

'Let me get you another drink,' he said after a good deal of this, and without waiting for an answer got up and strode off to the drinks cupboard. He was quite near Helene when, with perfect co-ordination, she turned towards the pool to say something to Macher's girl. This move presented her back to Roger and her front to where he had just been sitting. When he got back there with the drinks she had turned away again.

'Come on, you lot,' he called with a suddenness and an unlooked-for joviality that brought both Grace and Macher round in their seats. 'What about some action? Or are you all afraid of the water? Show us what you can do, eh?'

'We're not standing for that, are we, Nigel?' Joe roared. 'Let him see how wrong he is.' He moved along the diving-board, bony in a minimal pair of light green trunks. The group behind him began to break up.

'You're British, aren't you, Mr. Dean?' Macher asked loudly.

'I am. And the name is Micheldene.'

'I'm sorry. It has a hyphen in it, does it? Like Mitchell-Dean?'

'No no no, it's one word. Why, anyway?'

'Well now, I wouldn't know why, would I, Mr. Micheldene?'

'I fail to see who else would.'

'What? It's your name, isn't it?'

'What about it?'

'So you'd know why it's one word and I wouldn't.'

'I don't know what you're talking about.'

'Look, you asked me why your name was one word.'

'I did nothing of the kind. I asked you why you wanted to know if I were British.'

'Oh, that was what you asked me.' Macher laughed

quietly for a time while Roger watched him. 'I beg your
pardon. Well, the answer to that should be obvious enough.'
'Should it?'
'Yes. I wanted to know.'
'Just that?'
'Just that.'
'Thank you.'
'You're welcome.'

Roger had been suffering several kinds of pain during
this exchange. One was physical, the result of forcing his
eyeballs as far round to one side as they would go in hasty
attempts to get a look at Helene. More severe was the
emotional pain of not having got a look. Macher had kept
distracting his attention. By the time he had finished with
him all five of the bathing party were in the pool. A third
kind of pain got going in Roger. Retrospective in nature, it
came from not having reached out a foot and tipped
Macher, chair and all, into the water as soon as he opened
his horrible mouth.

The pool was not a long one, but it was sufficiently long
for Joe to think it worth while ploughing his way from
one end of it to the other again and again. Doing this made
him snort a lot. It also disturbed the water enough to turn
most of Helene, in the intervals when she was not herself
swimming, into a disintegrated mess of oscillating patches
of colour. There was the refraction too.

Ernst started to do some diving. He seemed good at it,
good enough at any rate to make Helene stop swimming
and watch him. Roger had a full close view of the back of
her head and shoulders. The water had altered the colours
of her hair, deepening the yellows, making the light parts
almost transparent and introducing bronze tints near the
crown. She and the others laughed and shouted to one
another in a relaxed, convivial way.

'Aren't they a lovely couple?' Grace asked Roger.

He gave her a suspicious glance. For a middle-aged
American woman she had not often struck him as very
unamiable, even though he had never contemplated bothering to find out what took place in her head. But he had
caught her eye late in the Macher monologue and found
her watching him interestedly, her nostrils dilated in a way
that meant she was suppressing something. A yawn, he
hoped. He said now in a puzzled tone: 'Who?'

'Why, Dr. and Mrs. Bang, of course. Don't you think
so?'

'Oh yes. Yes, I do. Quite charming.'

'They seem completely made for each other.'

'Yes.'

'If he ever decides he's done enough philosophy or whatever it is, I should imagine there must be a part waiting for
him in some Tarzan movie or other. He's so graceful. Look
at him go now. With those looks he might so easily be
effeminate, but there's nothing like that about him at all.
And isn't she just ravishing?'

'Oh, delightful.'

'So typically Scandinavian in her colouring. And that
figure. I really am surprised some fellow hasn't gotten hold
of her.'

'What sort of fellow?'

'Well, you know, some sort of movie or television fellow.
With those looks she wouldn't need to be able to sing or
anything, or even act.'

'No, she wouldn't, would she?'

'But you know what the loveliest part of all is.'

Roger gazed at her in unexpectant silence.

'They're so utterly devoted. You can see it the moment
you lay eyes on them the first time—well, I did. Completely devoted. He doesn't really care to look at anybody
else, and it's the same with her. Or even more so, wouldn't
you say?'

Roger would not say.

'And that's so rare these days, isn't it?—with all this running off and breaking up and divorcing and all the... Oh, I'm sorry, Roger, how terribly tactless of me. I didn't mean—'

'That's perfectly all right, Grace.'

'I do feel so—'

'Say no more.' Or else stand by for a dose of grievous bodily harm (Roger thought to himself), you women's-cultural-lunch-club-organising *Saturday Review of Literature*-reading substantial-inheritance-from-soft-drink-corporation-awaiting old-New-Hampshire-family-invoking Kennedy-loving just-wunnerful-labelling Yank bag.

Grace dropped her voice to say in a carefully casual tone: 'Did you hear anything from Marigold recently?'

'Not for some years.' Roger was aware of Macher listening to all this, and listening with something less than full attention too. That made it worse. If the Yid scribbler was going to go on sitting there with his lobeless ears flapping, Roger reasoned, the least he could do was flap them with passionate absorption. 'Marigold was my first wife,' he went on very loudly. 'My present wife, if you can call her that, is named Pamela.'

'Oh, Roger, I don't know what to say, I seem to have—'

'Sweetheart, it doesn't matter in the least.' He gave her a full-production smile to ram home his moral advantage. The grade-one going-over Grace had just earned would have to wait until he was unencumbered by the presence of Hebrew jackanapeses and such. 'I had a letter from Pamela just before I came over, actually.'

'How is she?'

'She seems very well.' Most of the single page of the letter had been devoted to asking him to see if he could find and bring back to England the unique typescript of a novel called *Perne in a Gyre* by his talentless nuclear-

disarmer brother-in-law. It was thought to be lying about
somewhere in the offices of a New York literary agent,
Strode Atkins by name, who was supposed to have been
attending this evening's gathering but had not, thank God,
so far appeared.

'Any real news?'

'No.'

Ernst had climbed out of the pool and stood pressing
the water from his hair. Helene, her back still turned to
Roger, was also emerging. Grace said she must see about
towels and went away. Roger watched Helene while she
chatted to her husband and to Macher's girl, accepted a
towel from Grace and moved round the pool to within a
few yards of him, the towel hiding most of her between the
neck and the knees. Her eyes were slightly bleared with the
water. After a moment she sat down, going so far as to
present Roger with a three-quarter rear view. Even though
the towel was round her shoulders and she was clasping
her knees, her shape was such that he got something. Not
enough, of course.

He was just rehearsing mentally the casualness with
which he would get up and walk over and ask her how she
had enjoyed her swim when Macher said: 'Some girl,
that.'

'Girl?' Roger went through the motions of noticing he
was not alone. 'What girl?'

'Not Suzanne Klein, the girl I brought. You haven't
noticed her. The other girl. The blonde. The Dane. The
professor's wife. Mrs. Bang. Helene. That girl.' He pointed.

'Oh yes, I think I see which one you're referring to.'

'Good. Some girl, isn't she?'

'Yes, I suppose you could say that.'

'I'm glad you agree. What's she like?'

'How do you mean?'

'Oh, you don't know how I mean.' Macher did his

laugh. 'Well now, let's just sit around for a while and get together and have a little think and try to figure out how I mean. I can't mean what's she like to look at, because I can see that for myself. As a matter of fact it was seeing what she's like to look at that led me to comment that she's some girl. Anyway, since we've decided I can't mean what's she like to look at I must mean something else, like is she nice or nasty, smart or stupid, educated or illiterate, drunken or of temperate disposition and habits—all this type of stuff. That's how I mean.'

Roger heard him out with unwavering gaze, his invariable policy in this situation unless a really murderous verbal interruption could be devised or physical violence resorted to. After prolonging his gaze for half a minute or so without speaking or moving, he said : 'I see. But quite apart from whether I feel I ought to consider giving you my opinion on these matters, I should have thought your approach to life in general was far too idiosyncratic for you to take an interest in what I or anyone else thought about this or anything else.'

'Oh no, Mr. Micheldene, that would be arrogant of me. You've misjudged me most terribly, I'm afraid. Of course I'm interested in what you think about Mrs. Bang. After all, you've known her much longer than I've had a chance to, haven't you? And you're an older man, so your judgment would be more mature and balanced than mine.'

'How true that is,' Roger said. 'However, allow me to suggest that we defer our discussion of Mrs. Bang until such time as you've acquired some basis of comparison. Until then at the very earliest.'

He was on his feet to go over and look at Helene's front when Grace called his name. He turned with some effort and saw her approaching across the grass with a man and a woman about his own age : Strode Atkins and his wife, no doubt. Both were of well-groomed and yet battered

appearance. They clearly expected to be introduced to him.
Roger was perplexed to find no red mist of rage clouding
his vision. He and Mrs. Atkins, a thin woman with large
eyes and straight brown hair done in a fringe, looked at
each other a moment longer than was necessary. Then her
husband was shaking his hand and shouting: 'An Englishman. Another goddam Englishman. I like that. I do like
that. I'm a horrible Anglophile, you know. And believe me
there aren't too many of them around these days, brother.'

CHAPTER III

'What sort of Anglophile's a horrible Anglophile?' Roger noticed that Mrs. Atkins was minutely studying an apparently featureless patch of grass not far from her feet.

'Oh hell, I just meant I love English people and English things so much it almost disgusts me. Disgusts a lot of other guys too, I can tell you. But I seem to keep right on doing it for some reason or other. What it is, I suppose, I'm of English descent. My ancestry is English. Goes back I don't know how far. Now I'd like to ask you something, Mr. Dean.'

'Micheldene.'

'I'm sorry—I'd like to ask you if you happen to be acquainted with the fact that the Tommy, the kind of, well, the English G.I. Joe, the average English private soldier, you know, like Uncle Sam as you know means the United States...uh...are you aware that the original Tommy was named Thomas Atkins?'

'Yes, now you mention it I do seem to remember hearing something of the sort.'

'Well, you can take it from me it's true. That'll show you how English I am. I'd like to ask you something else, too.'

'By all means.'

'How do you pronounce the word'—Strode Atkins frowned and licked his lips—'the word o, u, t?'

'Out,' Roger said without hesitation. The silent-stare ploy, just now tried on Macher with indifferent success,

would plainly not do at all here. 'Out,' he added for good
measure.

Atkins shook his head slowly and gravely. 'Oat,' he said
or something very like it.

'But people—'

Atkins held up his hand. 'How do you pronounce the
word'—he did some more frowning while he stared at his
feet, perhaps because he was rocking on them slightly—
'a, b, o, u, t?'

'About?'

Atkins sighed regretfully. 'Aboat.'

'But that's only the—'

'There are just two valleys in West Virginia in which
pure eighteenth-century English is spoken, English as it
used to be spoken in the eighteenth century. I come from
there. Now ... How do you—?'

Mrs. Atkins turned her head suddenly towards her husband and said with great conviction : 'Mr. Micheldene
isn't interested in playing word games. Why don't we all
go and sit down?'

'If you're looking for somebody to discuss pronunciations
with, Mr. Atkins,' Roger said jovially, 'I've got the very
man. Come and meet him.'

They went over carrying their drinks, Roger his fifth or
so, Atkins his first, at any rate since arriving. On the way
Roger found himself trying to explain who Ernst was and
what he did. He failed to hold his audience. When he was
five yards away from her Helene finished saying something
to Macher, got gracefully to her feet and walked off towards the changing-huts. Her hair had almost dried and
was stirring fluffily in the light breeze that had sprung up.

After uniting Bang and Atkins Roger wandered off by
himself. He looked round the large expanse of undulating
turf which the Derlangers called their yard. Its lack of
flower-beds and hedges gave it, for him, an unfinished

look. A low tree-covered hill half a mile distant showed off
the red and orange tints they all kept talking about. Apart
from this kind of thing and two or three scattered houses
there was nothing in the whole panorama to arrest the
eye. No vehicle moved on the road. At the base of a pine
on the far side of the drive a squirrel sat on its hind legs
and glanced about with affected curiosity. Then, with
affected urgency, it ran up the trunk, disturbing a scarlet
bird which flew energetically away towards the wood. The
Derlangers' Negro maidservant let the screen of the back
door bang behind her and went round the far side of the
house. Was all this worth the effort of close observation, of
an attempt at understanding? Roger thought not.

There was much else to occupy him. Before the evening
ended he had got to make some arrangement with Helene,
or at any rate an arrangement to make an arrangement.
Not for the first time he envied a chap in a French film he
had once seen. This chap had had a special lute thing on
which at suitable points he played a special chord. Its
effect was to reduce to senseless immobility everyone except
the lutanist and whichever young lady he had his eye on.
After retiring together for as long as they liked the pair
would resume their former positions and another chord set
life on the tramp again. Snappy little gadgets, those lutes,
but very hard to come by.

Short of a lute or a carefully placed hand-grenade
nothing suggested itself as a means of detaching Helene or
even of slowing the others down to a level where they could
be relied on not to rush up every fifteen seconds and start
discussing something. But get hold of her he must. The
next couple of weeks were going to give him his best
chance so far, perhaps his last, of taking Helene off somewhere, even for a couple of days. That would not be as
good as a couple of decades, but it would be better than
what he had had up to now: half a dozen bits of after-

noons and evenings in Copenhagen and London and a
large part of one night when Ernst had gone to Oxford to
read manuscripts. It hurt Roger that he could remember
so little of what he wanted to remember of that occasion.
All the rest was still vivid, the feigned departure (for
Arthur's benefit) from the rented Hampstead house, the
half-hour on the landing in stockinged feet while a wakeful
Arthur drank hot milk and had a story told, and the very
real departure at 5.45 a.m. while a reawakened Arthur
could be heard struggling to turn the knob of his bedroom
door. The couple of days must not feature Arthur.

However, Roger told himself now he would take on a
whole striking force of Arthurs if that couple of days could
be extended indefinitely. Was there any real hope of taking
Helene off Ernst? The last time in London she had promised to think about it and for once had kissed him on the
mouth when he saw them all off at the airport. And yet
her letter, arriving nearly a month afterwards, had been as
cheerful and as merely friendly as always. (And why had
she never learnt how to spell his name?) He had wanted to
ring her up and say what he so often wanted to say face
to face with her: *Look, you're supposed to be my mistress.*
It was not as if any rotten sod, or other rotten sod, were in
the running; he was pretty sure of that. What did she
really think of him?

Just then Helene came out from the huts, combing her
hair half-heartedly. It looked unusually fine and light. He
let off a short prayer that she had not really forgotten April
1961, had only been pretending for Ernst's benefit. Then
he went down the slope to join her. He slid about a bit in
doing so, either because of the gin or because he was holding his stomach in so tightly that his legs worked like stilts
or because the grass was slippery. He walked Helene along
to the house accompanied only by Suzanne Klein and Irving Macher and Strode Atkins and Nigel Pargeter. He

asked Helene if she had enjoyed her swim and she had time
to say yes before turning away to listen to what Macher
was saying about William Golding.

Indoors Grace won an argument with Joe, who wanted
them to eat in the yard, and led the women off upstairs.
Joe stood scowling for a moment before taking Atkins away
with him towards the domestic regions. Macher was also
missing, perhaps climbing a drainpipe to find out more
about what Helene was like to look at. Roger found himself
alone with Pargeter, who was about twenty-four and
bespectacled and very short in the leg and who said :

'Is this your first visit ?'

'To this house ?'

'No, to the United States.'

'No. Is it yours ?'

'Yes. I've only been here a couple of weeks. I was ill.'

'I'm sorry to hear that.'

'I'm in the graduate school at Budweiser.'

'Doing what ?'

'A Ph.D. thesis on Gavin Douglas.'

'What, that fifteenth-century Scotch bloke ?'

'Yes, do you know his work ?'

'He wasn't an American, was he ?'

'Of course not.'

'Then what the hell's the point of coming over here to
write about him ?'

'I didn't come over *to* write about him. I wanted to do
a Ph.D. and I got this studentship at Budweiser, so—'

'But aren't there manuscripts and stuff with a bloke like
Douglas ? You won't find those in Pennsylvania.'

'I'm not on that side of it.'

'Indeed ?' Roger said, and went out. He genuinely
wanted to go to the lavatory. Further, under pretext of
not knowing the house all that well he could wander
about a bit in the hope of running into Helene. He warned

himself that kissing her must take second priority to arranging when he could telephone her without risk of Ernst being about. Failing any of this, he might be lucky enough to come upon Macher doing something discreditable, pocketing a pre-Columbian *objet d'art* or being familiar with Suzanne Klein on a Dutch colonial day-bed.

In the event all he got to was the *jahn*. He paused in rebuttoning his trousers to take in the framed map of the world that hung on the wall. It had the Americas running down the middle, so that most other places were cut in half or appeared twice. How long would it be before they got UNO or something to shift the meridian of longitude so that it ran through Washington? And why—he glanced in the mirror—did Americans' faces not go nearly as red as his when they drank fully as much as he did?

Downstairs he was in time to see Joe striding with lowered head over to one of the pair of hearths that stood back to back halfway down the room, a pile of logs in his arms. These he let fall from chest height into the fireplace, afterwards booting the strays into position. Without looking up he said:

'If it's going to be as Christly cold as Grace seems to think, we'd better do something to keep from freezing to death. Now the kindling. There used to be some . . .'

Attentively watched by Roger and Pargeter, he was rummaging with most of his strength in a cupboard under a window-seat when Grace returned. 'Sweetheart, what on earth are you doing?'

'I was saying that since winter seems to have struck all of a sudden it's time we got a fire going. Then I'll start fixing a toddy, or perhaps a few hot buttered rums might—'

'Joe, you're crazy, darling, we'll roast in our seats with a fire. I didn't mean it was—'

'All right, so we'll open the windows.'

'Honey, really . . .'

Grace, hands clasped, stood shaking her neat waved head at her husband, who walked on his knees to the next cupboard and wrested it open. Pargeter moved over to Roger as if he very much wanted to discuss the weather with him. Then, with much rattling and clinking, Atkins came slowly in carrying a tray of drinks. The disposal of this, followed by the exertion of getting the plastic seal off the neck of a gin-bottle single-handed and equipped only with a sharp knife, seemed to drive the projected fire out of Joe's head.

When Helene reappeared she had Mrs. Atkins and Suzanne Klein and Macher with her. Macher was, and evidently had been for some time, talking about his novel.

'Their great fear,' he was saying as Roger came up, 'is spilling food down themselves, you see. As well as looking slovenly and sordid it advertises their condition. So in this blinkie joke-shop we have special sweaters with soup-stains down the—'

'Do forgive me,' Roger broke in, 'but what exactly is a blinkie joke-shop?'

'A joke-shop for blinkies, only they don't know it's a joke-shop. They think it's just a regular store with a few specialties in the way of . . . Oh, I'm sorry, Mr. Micheldene, I forgot you didn't hear what I said earlier. A blinkie is a blind person. And that's really a very descriptive term; it gets the fuss a lot of them make with their eyes, never letting them alone, opening and shutting them, screwing them up this sort of way,'—he demonstrated—'rubbing them and so on. Anyhow, in this store there are all sorts of things—blind seeing-eye dogs, cups for nickels with a sign saying *Take One*, and the dark-glasses counter is really something. All sorts of slogans painted in white on the lenses : *Screw You White Man* for Negro blinkies, and then an assortment of, oh, *God Damn All Kike Filth*, *Death to*

Lousy Irish Micks and so on, depending on the minorities situation in the district the guy comes from. Then for the favoured patron there's the girlie section—three-dimensional nudes, you know, very complete, four ninety-five, wth slogans as before. Across the back it says *Take Your Cotton-Picking Hands Off Me, You Blinkie Pervert,* and on the stomach there's—'

'But nobody would see that, would they?' Mrs. Atkins asked. 'It wouldn't be like the things painted on the glasses, which other people can—'

'But that's the whole point. Don't you see this makes it better? This way it's pure offensiveness, nobody getting any satisfaction out of it, all done for its own sake. Just the idea, nothing more. Like setting up a time-bomb in a children's hospital fixed to go off after you're dead. Wanting actual kicks from seeing it or hearing about it, that's weak and self-indulgent, that's being human, whereas what I'm concerned with—'

'Let's hear about the Black-Out,' Suzanne Klein said.

'I've renamed it the Blind Spot now. Oh, I don't know, Suzanne, perhaps we'd better leave that part. Maybe later.'

'What is the Blind Spot?' Helene asked.

'It's this blinkie burlesque joint,' Suzanne said, laughing in a carefree, extraverted way, 'where the strippers all have horrible faces, only of course the fellow who M.C.s the show builds them up as raving beauties. Go on, Irving.'

'Well...it's just when the girl with the biggest squint and the most acne is taking off her G-string that the hero gets his sight back, and naturally he's got everything—soup-stain sweater, *Screw You White Man* glasses, transparent pants ...'

'How does he get his sight back?' This was Helene again, listening to Macher as intently as if he were Ernst.

'The gods restore it to him, what else? Out of pity. They're always doing things like this. You remember that story by Chaucer where there's this blinkie oldster with the hot wife. It's really quite neat. He...'

Roger stopped listening to Macher's account of *The Franklin's Tale*. The fellow was earning a bigger and better punch-up, oral or physical, with every sentence he spoke, but it was too early yet for anything like that. Midnight, and extreme general drunkenness, were needed. And he must reconnoitre the enemy further before moving into the assault. Roger turned down the idea of a halting, puzzled question about whether all this stuff was meant to be *funny*. His tactical sense told him that Macher was more than ready for that one.

So he watched the women instead. Suzanne Klein's obvious attachment to her nasty escort depressed him. Although on the small side for his own taste, she was attractive, not as attractive as Helene, but still several times more attractive than her with-it off-beat far-out co-religionist deserved. Pretty women always tended to go for horrible men.

How was it, then, that Helene did not go for him, Roger, more heartily and continuously than she had done up to now? Most of the time, of course, he did not consider himself to be truly a horrible man. But it would have taken a far more self-deluding mind even than his not to notice that, to a superficial eye, Roger Micheldene Esq. was a bit more horrible than, say, Dr. Ernst Bang. And the trouble was that, like the rest of her sex, Helene had a superficial eye. This made it hard merely to get the chance of showing her the importance of things like, well, intellect and maturity and individuality.

He glanced intermittently and briefly at Helene. What he saw made him wish that there were no such thing as sex. He noticed that one of the lighter locks of hair had moved to the wrong side of the zig-zag parting. The white dress seemed to have shrunk a little in the last hour or two.

Alternatively, after it had been sprayed on to her she had been selectively blown up with a bicycle-pump. And here she was pretending to be just a woman enjoying herself.

Mrs. Atkins, at any rate, was making no such pretence. She stood in a slumped posture, dividing a not very attentive attention between her glass, Macher and, less often, her husband, who was now laughing almost without interval at the other end of the room. Her real interest, whatever it was, showed up in the periodic watchfulness that Roger thought he saw entering her wide-eyed gaze, though what if anything she was watching could not be placed. This look combined with her dejected, beaten air to remind Roger of someone. For the moment he had no idea who.

Dinner was announced, not a minute too soon for anybody who wanted to get to the table under his own power. As it was, Strode Atkins stumbled thoroughly three entirely separate times, once clutching at Roger's lapel for support, as the party made its way down a curving flight of stone stairs to the eating-room. Here curtains that Grace had said were folk-weave shut out whatever there was outside, with yellow candles burning in double-spiral pewter candlesticks. Above the wide hearth stood a lump of blueish stone that some Red Indian or Eskimo had battered into something like the shape of a man. The table-mats, instead of educating the guests with scenes from early sessions of Congress or maps of Pennſylvania with part of New Jerſey, were of plain linen. They interested Roger less than what was on them: gilt-rimmed plates bearing clam shells filled with hot crabmeat and breadcrumbs. This sight, and the thought that dinner-time was never much good for arranging to take people to bed, reconciled him to sitting between Ernst and Mrs. Atkins at the far end of the table from Helene.

Roger began eating. There was a roll-basket on the table

near him, its contents hidden by a napkin. Underneath this were lengths of hot Italian bread soaked in garlic butter. He decided he would not eat this, and then suddenly found he had started to. His decision to eat only one piece went the same way. By the time the Southern fried chicken arrived from the gloved hand of the Negro maid it was plain to him that he might as well be hung for a fat-tailed sheep as a lamb. With the chicken there were turnips, spring onions—no point in refusing them after the garlic—and corn on the cob with more butter. A razor-blade embedded in a wooden handle for slicing the cobs and a paintbrush affair for spreading the melted butter on them were passed from hand to hand. Roger used both instruments a lot.

While Ernst and Pargeter, who was sitting opposite, filled him in on what terrible courses of study were available at Budweiser, Roger concentrated on his food. It was the least he could do for something that was bringing his coronary nearer at such a clip, that was already, he sensed, sidling irremovably into his paunch and his neck and his bosom. Let it. As he waited for his helping of blueberry pancakes with fresh cream and Wisconsin cheddar, the thought of dieting brushed feebly at his mind like an old remorse. He was aware that just eating a little of what he did not fancy would sooner or later do him good in the sexual chase. This idea had been brought sharply into focus at a fellow-publisher's party the previous year. Somebody's secretary had told him that what he wanted was all right with her on the understanding that he brought his block and tackle along. Five days later, sipping a half-cup of sugarless milkless tea to round off a luncheon of a lightly boiled egg with no salt, a decarbohydrated roll resembling fluff in plastic, and a small apple, he had made up his mind for ever that, if it came to it, he could easily settle down to a regime of banquets and self-abuse. He sent

his plate up now for a second helping of pancakes and put
three chocolate mints into his mouth to tide him over.
Outside every fat man there was an even fatter man trying
to close in.

With the Gaelic coffee, surmounted by half an inch or
so of chilled cream, he felt his survival till breakfast
guaranteed and accepted a cigar ceremoniously produced
for him by Joe. It turned out to be a perfectly ordinary
Manila, a little hot in the mouth, but airy, well-rolled, and
with no beastly Brazilian leaf in it. The first couple of
inches should be quite smokable. Waving away a lighter
and calling for a match, he lent an ear to Pargeter's an-
guished account of a Budweiser freshman programme
called World Literature 108. He added the other ear when
Pargeter said:

'By the way, I've got a message for you from Maynard
Parrish.'

'Oh, that old nitwit. What does he want?'

'Isn't he a friend of yours? He seemed to think—'

'We did his book on Melville and I couldn't get out of
seeing something of him last year. What does he want?'

'He wondered if you'd be interested in giving a talk to
the English Club. Next Friday would be the—'

'Why doesn't he ask me, then?'

'He asked me to see if you were interested. Then if you
are he'll write to you, you see.'

'Yes, I see. Well, I don't really think . . .'

'They pay a hundred dollars, I should have said.'

'Oh.'

'Something on the book trade in Britain and America,
Parrish thought.'

'Mm.'

'You must come, Roger,' Ernst said. 'Say you will. You'll
stay with us, of course. We can easily put you up.' He
leant forward animatedly. 'Stay the weekend. We'll have

a party. Helene. Helene, darling, Roger will be coming for
next weekend to stay with us. Isn't that a good idea?'

First laughing and saying something to Joe, Helene
looked over and said it was, then turned back to Joe.

'That's settled, then,' Ernst said. 'You can come down
from New York in the afternoon—there's an excellent train
service, and you needn't go back till Monday. First-rate.
Get on to Parrish straight away, Nigel. I promise you we'll
all have the most marvellous time.'

CHAPTER IV

Roger's elation at the way things had turned out
lasted an hour or two. He had been determined to get himself into the Bangs' house even if it had meant breaking
their door down, but this method was better. He would
always cherish the memory of his own acceptance of the
invitation: surprised, grateful, calculating whether he could
fit it in. He did not even scowl when Joe, after waiting for
the sobering effects of the meal to wear off, proposed they
played the Game.

'The Game?' Pargeter asked in wonder.

'Well, this is a kind of alternate form of it,' Joe
explained. 'You have to guess an adverb.'

'Any adverb?'

'Well yes, it can be almost any adverb, but it's the one
we act. We all act the adverb in turn.'

'Which adverb?'

'Naturally there are some that wouldn't be any good,
like *often* and *sometimes*. They are adverbs, aren't they?
Ernst would know. Where's he gone?'

'I'm afraid you'll have to—'

'Joe means we send someone out of the room,' Grace
said, 'and the rest of us decide on an adverb, like *proudly*
or *uninterestedly* or *lecherously*—that's if Joe has any say
in the choice, and then we call the guy in and he says to
each of us one after the other, "Go polish that mirror or
light a cigarette or wind your watch in the way indicated,"
and after a while he guesses the word.'

Pargeter frowned. 'How would you wind your watch lecherously?'

'You wait till you see Joe working on it. Last time we played he blew his nose adulterously. It's all right, you'll catch on.'

Perhaps Pargeter did in some inner recess of his mind, but when it came to his turn he watched Strode Atkins hopping round the room (and twice bouncing off the wall) energetically and Grace folding up a rug energetically and Suzanne Klein putting on lipstick energetically before saying: 'Incredibly.' Soon after that they told him.

Then it was Helene's turn. While her adverb was being selected Roger dallied with thoughts of a variation on the present game. In it, Helene would act a special set of adverbs for him to guess. Nobody else would be about. He lent judicious support to Joe's final suggestion of *passionately*. Having stationed himself nearest the door for the purpose, he was elected to go and fetch Helene, or rather had bolted from the room before anybody had thought of simply yelling her name.

She was looking at college groups in the sort of study where Joe worked at weekends if he worked at all. Roger grabbed her instantly. All things considered she reacted well to having sixteen stone of drunken garlic-breathing Englishman flung at her. Only when she was in grave danger of collapsing backwards on to Joe's recording machine did she wriggle free. And even in that short space of time she had made it clear that her Certificate of Oral Proficiency, once mentioned on an occasion when matters French were under discussion, had not been awarded in error.

Panting a bit, working hard on lipstick-removal, Roger managed to get out a question about when he could telephone her.

'Oh, any time at all.'

'You mean . . . Listen, darling, when can I telephone you when Ernst won't be about?'

'But what'll you want to say? Can't you tell me now?'

'I . . . I want to arrange to see you.'

She looked at him with just a hint of puzzlement. 'But you can come around any time, and anyway you'll be seeing me next weekend.'

'I mean see you on your own, damn it, so that we can . . . Quick now. When? When can I phone you, Helene?'

'We should get back in, shouldn't we?'

'For Christ's sake, Helene, when can I phone you?'

'Oh, any time . . . All right, between nine and ten in the morning is usually okay.'

'I'll phone you at nine-thirty on Monday. Now you go in. I'll dash upstairs. See you soon, darling.'

Roger got as near dashing as he normally let himself get after eating something like five per cent of his unloaded weight. On this visit he regarded the centralised Americas with more tolerance. A continent where he and Helene were going to get together had something to be said for it.

Back at the centre of things he found Helene composedly watching Pargeter, who, with a good deal of coaching from everybody else, was trying to drink his highball passionately. Roger promised himself he would give her full value, but in the event had to do his best with reading aloud passionately part of an article in a handy copy of *Life*. 'Laos is a storm-centre,' he croaked, goggling at Helene's bosom, 'in a region traditionally long on storm-centres.' He broke off now and again to snort and quiver. But it was no good really.

After a time Helene was agreed to have got near enough to make no difference. Then it was Roger's turn. He had hardly left the room before Macher recalled him to it. This struck him as ominous. So did the way they all grinned at him.

He decided to get it over quickly. 'Examine yourself in the glass like it,' he said to Joe.

Wiggling his bottom, Joe strolled over to the mirror above the nearer hearth. He clasped his hands behind his head and smiled at himself, put his hands on his hips and frowned and pouted, smoothed his eyebrows with moistened fingertips.

'Effeminately,' Roger said.

There was laughter, especially from Macher and Suzanne. 'Not really,' Macher said.

'Not too far off, though,' Strode Atkins said.

Reactions were similar when Grace minced round the room wielding an imaginary feather duster and Roger said : 'Haughtily.'

'That's part of it too,' Atkins said.

At Roger's bidding Ernst emptied ashtrays into a waste-paper basket. His movements were swift and decisive, his face without expression. When he had finished he turned to Roger and gave a curt nod.

'Efficiently.'

'No, you're getting right away from it now,' Atkins said.

'Helene,' Roger said. He could put it off no longer. 'Make love to that standard lamp like it.'

She thought a moment, then marched like a Guardsman in the direction named. Roger, who had a front view of her for once, fully appreciated this unforeseen bonus. Arrived at the lamp, she seized the brass pillar in both hands, bestowed a single token peck on the shade, turned about and strode back to her starting-point. All the others laughed and applauded, looking at Roger rather than at Helene.

'I don't know,' Roger said. 'Severely. Chastely. Masculinely. You all seem to be doing different words.'

'Shall we tell him ? He'll never get it.'

'Yes, why not ? Go ahead and tell him.'

Helene faced Roger. 'Britishly,' she said.

Roger's eye held hers. She smiled cheerfully and un-maliciously at him. There was a feeling in his head, neck and chest as if pockets of warm air were gradually expanding. It was how rage usually took him. 'Who thought of it?' he asked very slowly. 'You?'

'No, actually it was me,' Pargeter said.

'Oh, it was, was it? And what was the precise nature of the appeal the notion held for you?'

'Sorry?'

'What was the idea?'

'Oh, I thought it would be amusing.'

'Permit me to congratulate you on your taste in humour.'

'I just thought it would be interesting to see what mannerisms and things struck Americans as typically British. Sort of a new light on how they felt about us.'

'Oh, fascinating. And so vitally necessary, new light on that. Well, I trust you're satisfied with the results of your little field study?'

'Oh yes, I thought it was most—'

'However, I'm afraid you'll have to excuse me from taking any further part in your sociological investigations. Good-night.'

Helene, with a troubled expression, took a pace towards him and said: 'Oh, please, Roger.' He ignored her.

Joe barred his path to the door. 'Oh, come on, Rog, don't be huffy. Have a drink. Don't break up the party.'

'I fail to see how my departure can adversely affect the possible—'

'Oh, crap. Fail to see. Adversely affect. The guy was fooling. We all were. This is supposed to be a game, for Christ's sake. What are you trying to prove? Oh, all right, hell, have it your way, see if I care.'

Roger went and stood at the french windows in the study. Eventually his ample chest slowed its rise and fall.

Meanwhile the party was indeed breaking up, not coming to an end but relaxing its cohesion. Roger heard voices shouting and laughing at different distances. He became aware that Mrs. Atkins was standing near him, a drink in her hand. She gave him her watchful look. Immediately he knew exactly who she reminded him of : any and every one of a dozen or so women he had run into in the past year or so. Heavy breathing made itself heard behind him. Strode Atkins, he saw, was standing a couple of yards inside the threshold raising his drink to his mouth. When it got there he reeled backwards out of sight as if hit in the face. From the hall came the sound of a heavy body striking furniture, then silence.

Roger turned to Mrs. Atkins and jerked his head towards the windows. 'Out,' he said in a drill-sergeant's tone. 'Or, if you prefer it, oat.'

What happened next happened somewhere down by the swimming-pool. That was all Roger was really sure of afterwards, that and the fact that it had happened. Oh yes, and he fancied there had been a lot of talking going on during it, much more than usual, and of an unfamiliar kind.

Ten or fifteen minutes later, or quite possibly two minutes or an hour later, he was standing in the light from one of the windows trying to write down a telephone number and the address of what seemed to be a shop. He noticed that the grass looked unexpectedly green. Then he realised that he was confronted by a re-entry problem as acute in its way as any astronaut's. 'You go back that way,' he said into the darkness. 'I'll go round to the front.'

There were no snags, none obvious enough for him to notice, anyway. In what Joe called the talking-room Roger was surprised to see Atkins on his feet still, or again, holding a drink and talking to Macher. Tactical instinct took him straight over to them. Macher glanced at Roger indulgently. 'I'd like that,' he said to Atkins.

'Any time at all, kid,' Atkins said. 'We hardly use the place. Just stop by at the office and pick up the key.' He put his hand carefully on Macher's shoulder and addressed Roger. 'Young fellow like this needs a place in the big city where he can take a bath or a nap or change his clothes, know what I mean?' He winked, using a lot of face. 'Mitch knows what I mean, don't you, Mitch? Youth. Youth will be served, right, Mitch? And not only youth, either. Old Mitch has been served before now, eh, Mitch? Helps himself all the time. I'm for that. When old Mitch moves in for the kill—whoo! Old wham-bam-thank-you-mam Mitch. You know, Irving, my old friend Mitch isn't as bad as he looks. Little bit stiff and formal, sure, but we all have our weaknesses, don't we?'

'He showed up very well at the end of that hilarious game.' Macher appeared entirely sober. 'He was good then.'

'In what way good?' Roger asked, glaring only slightly.

'You behaved without thinking. You did what you wanted to do. You should try it more often. It works. And it's your duty.'

'Duty? What the devil are you talking about?'

'Human life is so horrible,' Macher said, as if wearily but good-humouredly expounding the self-evident, 'that the only thing to do is do what you want. Any means are justifiable for getting what you want, up to and including murder.'

'Is this supposed to be new?' Roger picked up an unattended drink and began drinking it.

'Who cares whether it's new? What matters is whether it's right. And it is right.'

'I should very much dislike living in that kind of world.'

'But it's the world you do live in. It's just you don't realise it.'

'I'd wager any sum you care to name that I'm at least

as selfish as you are, but I must confess I'm unable to see
the need of working the whole thing up into a philosophy.'

Macher's manner remained as friendly when he said:
'Utter nonsense. It isn't working anything up into anything to describe a situation correctly and deduce a plan
for dealing with it. There's no rain in a week and the
grass needs water so you water it. And this isn't selfish in
the way you probably mean. We all have people we like
and love. It's our duty to steal and cheat and lie and use
violence whenever it's necessary to look after these people.'

'Here's another of our guests from across the sea.' Atkins,
after listening with puzzled disgust to the start of Macher's
exposition, had wandered off. He now returned, dragging
with him Pargeter, who until just then had been sitting
on an oak settle with his face in his hands. 'You homesick
yet, old boy?'

'Good God, no,' Pargeter half-yelled. 'What, homesick
for that bloody awful dump?'

'There you are, he's one of us already,' Atkins said,
beaming.

'What did you say your name was?' Roger asked. 'Pargeter or something?'

'Nigel Pargeter.'

'Well, Pargeter, I'm afraid I don't understand you.'

Macher laughed. 'Confess yourself unable to understand
him as it were—isn't that more your style, Mr. Micheldene? But seriously, you have a lot of trouble with these
matters of communication, don't you? Kind of a recurrent
problem.'

Roger ignored this. 'Come on, Pargeter, how is England
a bloody awful dump?'

'Oh, I'm sure it's all right for you, Mr. Micheldene
Esquire, with your expensive accent and your...Not for
poor sods like me, though. Class distinction and the old-boy
network and the Queen and the Archbishop of Canterbury

and Eton and the telly and the affluent society and materialism and . . . well . . .'

'Oh, I've got you now, Pargeter, you're one of these
beastly little—'

'No values, no sense of—'

'You've picked a funny place to come to if you want to
get away from materialism and the affluent society, haven't
you, Pargeter? And class distinction. I suppose you think
that just because there aren't any dukes here everybody's
all chums together. Complete illusion. Look, when the
Queen and Prince Philip were here and drove through
New York or Washington or one of these places they had
more of a reception than that frightful man General Mac-
Arthur. More popular than a national—'

'No, a good deal less popular,' Macher said. 'To be
precise, between one-quarter and one-fifth as popular.'

'Well, that's a marvel of American scientific know-how,
to be sure,' Roger said happily. 'So you've learnt how to
measure popularity, eh?'

'In this situation, yes. When these processions pass,
people throw ticker-tape and suchlike out the windows on
to the—'

'Ticker-tape, ticker-tape? What a—'

'I'm sorry, Mr. Micheldene, but whether you like it or
not it's called ticker-tape. Anyhow, when the streets are
cleaned afterwards the New York City Department of
Sanitation weighs the ticker-tape, and—I've forgotten how
many tons are involved or where I saw the figures, but I
remember noticing that your Queen and Prince rated
between one-quarter and one-fifth as much as that (I agree)
frightful man MacArthur.'

Pargeter, whose occasional yelped half-syllables had
shown he was trying to get back in, managed to when
Roger found nothing to say for the moment. 'Christ,' he
howled at Roger, 'you don't think I take that line on the

States, do you? Do you think I don't know it's a bloody
sight worse than England in all these ways? Bloody gold-
plated bathroom taps and the John Birch Society and
muggings in Central Park and no Jews in the golf club and
Little Rock and Las Vegas and Vassar and . . . well . . .
If it was my own country I'd simply . . .'

A tricky regrouping seemed in store for Roger, but
Atkins now said pleadingly : 'Mitch, listen to me.' He put
his face near and his arm round Roger's shoulders, using
the other hand to wave Pargeter down. 'Mitch, I'd like
to ask you something. Come on now, listen. Why do you
hate us?'

'Hate you? How do you mean? I mean—'

'Why do you hate us? You do, don't you? You all do.
Why? Why? What have we done to you? We didn't want
to be world leaders. Last thing we wanted. We've never
been imperialist. And yet you hate us. Why? We've never
been colonialist. And yet you—'

'Oh, really?' Roger snapped into action again, going the
faster to obviate the insult of Pargeter's support. 'Never
been imperialist or colonialist? What about the Mexican
War and the Spanish War? Why do you think places like
California and Arizona and Florida and Puerto Rico and
the rest of them have got those curious foreign-sounding
names? And the South—the only reason it's not called a
colony is because it's within the—'

'Mitch, Mitch, Mitch,' Atkins broke through by degrees,
'I'm a horrible Anglophile. And you're trying to change
me, boy.'

'Nobody could change you, you dull bastard,' Roger said.

Atkins had taken his arm away and now stood shrug-
ging and swaying. 'No, I guess nobody could,' he said. He
started grinning, his eyes on the floor. 'No, Mitch, I guess
you're in the right of it there.'

Roger looked up and met Helene's glance. It was fixed

directly on him for the first time that evening, and was full of contempt. She left the room and he followed.

'What's the matter with you, Roger? Are you sick or something? Insulting that nice funny little man? Why are you always like this? Oh, God, it's so awful. I'm about through—I don't think I can stand it any more. Oh, what makes you behave this way?'

'You dare lecture to me on how to behave after that perfectly monstrous exhibition of yours earlier on? Insulting me and my country in front of everyone? The most preposterous—'

'Roger, are you insane? Are you literally, certifiably insane? Don't you know a joke when you see one? Where's that jolly old sense of humour the British are supposed to have?'

'Ha, that's even better, isn't it? A Dane laying down the law on humour. Talk about—'

'I'm no Dane, damn you, I'm American.'

'That's a matter of opinion, darling.' Ernst walked buoyantly over with a glass of milk in his hand. He looked as if he had just showered after a brisk early-morning run. 'But we won't pursue it now. Have I been missing something, Roger? Some fisticuffs?'

'Everything but,' Helene said, gazing furiously at Roger. 'Let's get home, Ernst. If we don't break it up there'll be an economy-size slugfest in a little while.'

'Yes, it is late. Well, Roger, things always start to hum when you're about, don't they? Never a flat moment, eh?'

Roger only calmed down finally when he stood in his bedroom tying the cord of his orange-and-black silk pyjamas. The seven dinner-guests had gone without his having been able to get near Helene again. He was leadenly visualising tomorrow morning's round of penitential phone-calls when Joe knocked and came in carrying a thick cardboard file.

'Young Macher's novel,' he said. 'I thought you might care for some bedtime reading.'

'How thoughtful of you.'

'I gathered you had a kind of passage of arms with Strode.'

'Insufferable little swine.'

'Yeah, I know, he can be hard to take at times. He has his problems, though. Like the rest of us. And don't underrate him, Rog. He's a real smart cookie.'

'Smart? Are you serious? Man's a moron.'

'Yeah, I know about that too, but there's a lot there that doesn't show. That manuscript business of his, he makes a lot out of that now. The agency's getting to be almost a sideline. Last year alone—'

'I know a bit about that sideline. He's been sitting on the typescript of a novel by my brother-in-law for God knows how long. I'll have to get it off him somehow.' At the moment Roger meant this. Since coming upstairs he had thought quite a bit about Pamela and the possibility of a reconciliation.

Full of American energy, or American inability to retire to one's bed, Joe settled himself on Roger's and opened a new packet of cigarettes. A few seconds' furious finger-flicking at the base of this got the first cigarette up far enough to be torn free and lit. Then Joe started: 'The whisper is—this is between ourselves, Rog—Strode's got his hands on some notebooks of Swinburne. Not very legally —three guys in England say the things belong to some library somewhere but they don't know where to look for them. Strode's supposed to be waiting for them to cool off so that he can push them to some fellow who likes that type of stuff. You know, whipping and the rest of it.'

'Yes, I know.' Roger, his back to Joe, had finished openly rubbing hair-tonic into his scalp and was now furtively rubbing skin-tonic round his eyes.

'Never seemed a good idea to me, being whipped,' Joe
said in some surprise. 'Other things, maybe, but not that.
Just once or twice I've thought when I was stoned to hell
I might like to sample it for the experience, but Jesus, the
first time that lash curled round my bare ass would be
enough to . . . You ever been whipped, Rog?'

'Not my line, old boy.'

'They say Swinburne got the taste for it at his prep
school. British schools have always been big on flogging,
haven't they? Raises an interesting point. The basic psycho-
logical situation here is getting ideas of sex muddled up
with ideas of violence, tenderness inverted into cruelty,
right? Now a lot of people would say this is, you know,
very much a British thing, and I'm wondering just how
far—'

'My dear Joe, I don't want to be rude but I am very
tired and I have to be up early in the morning, so perhaps
we could continue this—'

'Sure, Rog, of course, I was forgetting, sorry. We'll see
you at breakfast, then. Good-night.'

Roger wound and set his alarm-clock and put it by the
bed. Then he knelt down on a zebra-hide rug, crossed
himself, and muttered:

'*In nomine Patris, Filii, et Spiritus Sancti.* Now look, this
isn't good enough. You know what I'm like and yet you
keep on at me. All those people—you know as well as I do
they're the type I can't stand. Why do you keep sending
along bastards like Atkins and Macher and bloody fools
like that Pargeter creature if you don't want me to be
angry? When a chap starts talking the sort of pretentious
cock that horrid little—'

Conscious that his voice had risen, he paused and went
on in his mutter: 'And what makes you think I need
showing how one sin leads to another? I knew that when I
was thirteen. That Mrs. Atkins business tonight—it was

wrong and I hereby repent it and beg pardon, but I wouldn't have done it if you hadn't made me angry. Hadn't made it easy for me to be angry, I mean. Please, if I felt you were showing a little restraint I'd be able to try much harder.

'Then there's Helene. Of course the whole thing's very wrong and I shouldn't be asking you to let me commit a sin, but won't you let me arrange something? If you only would I could get it all cleared up: I'll take her away and marry her, or else I'll stop seeing her. Either way I shan't be going on like this, which I agree is very bad. I'm only asking for this one chance. You must know how much I want it, for Christ's sake.'

Roger stayed on his knees for half a minute or so. Then he added out of the corner of his mouth: 'And whatever you do see to it that Irving Macher's novel is no good.'

He climbed to his feet effortfully and with clicking knee-caps. A bird called outside, an ugly and unfamiliar sound. A blue jay, or one of the other local sorts they kept on about. He got into bed, clutching at the quilt as, with its usual promptness, it started sliding off. What frightful toll such a quilt must take of Joe if he had one on his own bed, Roger reflected, and if so how inevitable that Joe should refuse to replace it with another, more adhesive type of quilt. That would be cheating destiny.

Once more grabbing the quilt, Roger got out of bed again and tramped to the wardrobe where his jacket was. He took from a pocket his folder of traveller's cheques and peered at the scribblings on it. *Plaza restaurant 1.0 p.m. Tuesday*—Christ, was that it? No, thank Christ, he remembered now—bloke from Doubleday's. Ah: *Miranda, Fothergill Street, Ammanford, WAlnut 6-4077.* That looked like it, both in content and in (barely legible) calligraphy. But what the hell was the woman's name? And what sort of face had she?

CHAPTER V

'PLEASE LET ME go, Roger. Please.'

'Nonsense.'

'Roger, will you let me up, please?'

'Why on earth should I?'

'Look, I told you we're having some people in for cock-tails this evening and I just remembered we're fresh out of vermouth and we're low on bourbon too, and I have to call the liquor store before three o'clock or they won't deliver this far out of town, and it's a quarter of already, so unless—'

'So you needn't move for at least ten minutes. Darling . . .'

'Oh . . . why can't you be reasonable?'

'I don't feel reasonable.'

'But you're going to be it just the same, aren't you? It won't take me two minutes to call and then I'll be right back.'

'I shall time you. I warn you I shall time you.'

'You do that. Now if you'll just—'

'I want a kiss first.'

'Oh, for heaven's sake . . .'

'You're saying good-bye to me. For two minutes. No more.'

'All right . . . Now I have to go . . . Oh, don't start that again.'

'Can I come with you and help you telephone? I'm good at that.'

'Maybe you are, but you're staying right there. It'll be a hell of a sight quicker, for one thing.'

'Ah, now in that regard I think it more than probable that you have a point. Just one more little . . .'

'Oh, honestly . . .'

As soon as Roger finally let her go Helene jumped up from his lap and stalked across to the kitchen door, combing her hair briefly with her fingers. Watching her go, Roger felt complacent, partly through having just drawn a little-considered benefit from being fat. A lap as wide and deep as his could accommodate indefinitely a girl far bulkier than Helene, in fact a girl of any standard size and weight. And a lap was a good place to put a girl. She felt safer there for some reason, but was not. There was something masterful as well about the idea of a lap.

The abdominal boundary of Roger's lap was at the moment even more convex than usual. On its further side weltered a dozen clams, a soft-shell crab with beans and egg-plant, a double order of apple pie and whipped cream, much pumpernickel and butter, and a bottle of New York State champagne. Roger was always frightfully good on this last sort of thing, very tolerant, and very funny at the expense of all that stuff about burgundies of great breeding and finesse. If it made him drunk without making him throw up on the spot, he would declare, it was his drink. The company would thus be nicely in position when, the meal over, he asked to see every brand of cigar they had in the place, looked at three, smelt one, sent all away, and got going on his snuff-boxes.

Today's cigar demonstration at the Queen's Tavern had been on a reduced scale—nobody to notice besides a few other lunchers and Helene, and there was probably little hope of impressing her further in this direction. She could not have forgotten—who could?—the time at the Hotel Codan when, staring woundingly into the waiter's eyes, he had crushed out a 17kr.50 Corona Corona after half a dozen puffs. In the ensuing hush he had explained, without any rancour now, that owing to carelessness on the part of the finisher the wrapper was cracked and the head—as the end you stuck in your mouth was correctly known—therefore imperfect. As he talked he had felt great waves of power flooding in towards him. There had been a seventh wave when he smilingly declined the fervent offer by the management of any other cigar he fancied (estimating accurately that when the bill came the offending weed would not appear on it).

Though of low cigar interest it had been a good lunch. Its only defect had been the time it took place. So as to get Helene back to the Bangs' house as early as possible, Roger had been willing to start eating at noon, or even 11 a.m., but she had told him over the telephone that, with an appointment for a Swedish massage at 10.30 and 'a few things' to buy at the supermarket afterwards, she could not be at the station to pick him up before about 12.30. Faced with the choice of arriving there at 11.53 or 12.44, he had gone for the earlier train and was very ready to see her when she turned up at 12.50. He had not been able to push the necessary two large martinis into her in less than a quarter of an hour, and the meal itself, like all meals, was not to be rushed. With the evil presence of Arthur, back from school, forecast for 4.0, they had the house to themselves for just about the next hour.

Roger became conscious that Helene had stopped talking a minute or more ago, but that she had not rejoined him. Instead of that, kitchen noises were coming from the kitchen : cupboards, drawers, crockery. Coffee. How nice; but how readily postponable.

He strolled the length of the room, glancing out of the picture window which gave so oddly little illumination. A small deer was moving slowly and without evident timidity through a belt of conifers thirty yards away. This sight caused Roger definite annoyance. He was not clear in his mind how he wanted these people to regard the fauna of their country, but he could have done with less of their habit of hanging up an Audubon print wherever they felt like it and less of their excited wonder at harbouring so many species within their borders. It stood to reason that any fool who owned half a continent was going to own a lot of birds and mammals and such as well. They ought to have got over all that by now.

Mildly ill-wishing the American deer, Roger turned a corner and did his best to peer impishly round the kitchen threshold. (The place was one of those ranch-type affairs that of course left doors off to promote togetherness.) 'And what do you think you're up to?' he asked in what he thought of as his jocular-sinister manner.

She turned her unkempt head towards him in faint surprise. So far from preparing coffee she seemed to be wrapping up small parcels and sweets and nuts in squares of orange paper. 'I have to do this,' she said.

He advanced on her. 'What? Do what?'

'The kids'll be coming around for trick-or-treat and I have to—'

'What?'

'It's Hallowe'en, Roger, and we always—'

'What of it?'

'I have to get these—'

By this time he had her cornered somewhere among the vast banks of domestic apparatus. Interlocked, they slid along the smooth white door of the man-high refrigerator and came to rest against the dishwasher, or perhaps the spin-drier. There was relative silence for a minute or so. Then Helene said:

'The Selbys might see us from across the yard—we shouldn't be—'

'All right, we'll go back and sit down.'

'But I should finish wrapping the—'

'Later. Whatever it is and I don't know or care what it is, later.'

He got her in a sort of policeman's come-along hold and assisted her to their seat in the main room. After another minute or so she began to resist him.

'It's all right, darling,' he said.

'No it isn't all right. Who says it's all right?'

'Don't be so silly. Of course it's all right.'

He wondered if they would ever reach a stage at which it became unnecessary for him to seduce her *de novo* every time. It had always been well worth it but the prospect of an indefinite series of these preambles, neither lengthening nor shortening, had begun to daunt him rather, and also disturb him. What was he doing that he ought not to do, or not doing that he ought to do? He was sure he had not deviated an inch from the standard procedure which, if successful at all, could normally be dispensed with after the first application. What was wrong with her? Did Ernst have to ply her with flowers, drinks, dinners, speeches whenever he felt like getting conjugal?

Blurring his voice, he said now: 'Let's go to bed.'

'No, Roger.'

'Why not?'

'We can't.'

Her tone had moved from her ordinary reluctance to decision. 'Why not?' he repeated, this time in real inquiry.

'We just can't. Arthur'll be here any time now.'

'But it's only . . . a quarter past three. He's not due till four.'

She shook her head rapidly. 'Any time now.'

'But you said on the phone . . .'

'I told you, it's Hallowe'en.'

'What the devil has that got to do with it?'

'They . . . they'll probably let them out of school early today, so they can get home and dress up for the evening.'

'Why the hell didn't you tell me? Christ, Helene.'

'Don't be angry, honey, please . . . Monday I told you he got home around four, and on regular days he does. Then when you called today you were so set on coming I just didn't have . . . time to tell you this wasn't a regular day, that's all.'

'My God, if I'd known . . .'

'If you'd known then what?'

Roger brooded, swallowing heavily. 'Listen. Are you sure he's coming home early?'

'Well, I'm pretty sure. It got mentioned . . .'

'How early?'

'I don't know, but what difference—?'

'Let's telephone the school and find out.'

'All right,' Helene said, getting slowly to her feet. 'We'll telephone the school.'

They got the janitor, who was very affable but knew nothing. Helene had some trouble getting the receiver back on to the hook before Roger could demand to speak to someone in authority.

Standing face to face with her in the kitchen, he wiped his mouth with the back of his hand. 'How's he getting home?'

'Well, we have this taxi group . . .'

'Taxi group? Talk English, Helene, do you mind?'

'We take turns, the mothers, the ones on this street. Once or twice a week one of us has a turn to take them to school and go fetch them.'

'Whose turn is it today?'

'Let's see . . . I think it must be Sue Green. But honey, look, even if—'

'Ring her up and ask her what time they come out.'

'But we couldn't possibly have more than—'

'Ring her up.'

Helene looked blankly at him for a moment, then dialled. 'Hallo? Hallo, is this Linda? Hi, honey, this is Helene? Oh, I'm fine. Say, is Mommy around? She did? No, it's nothing. We'll see you soon. Good-bye now.' She added to Roger: 'Sue already left.'

'So I gather, but how long ago? I mean, God . . . Why didn't you ask?'

'Linda Green is four years old,' Helene said.

'What? There must be someone else in the house, mustn't there?'

She shook her head, not in negation, and turned away. With a hand on her upper arm he pulled her round again to face him.

'Don't you try that with me, young woman. You listen to what I have to say. What kind of a game do you think you're playing with me? Why do you think I came down all this way today, total of four hours in the train and the rest of it? To have lunch with you and then sit and hold your bloody hand? Clearly not. I came here to go to bed with you, only it appears that owing to an unfortunate oversight on your part I am to be debarred from doing so. Not that that impinges on your well-being to the remotest degree. Quite the contrary, in fact. I know what you're about and I know you. You look lecherous but actually you're not in the least—you haven't a particle of ordinary sinful human sensuality in your whole body. But allow me to inform you that there are far worse sins than lechery. Pride is what possesses you and eats you away, pride and the love of power.'

He looked at her and saw that, although her eyes were still blank, her mouth was half open and she was breathing quickly. 'You're cold,' he shouted; then, after a pause, added in a broken voice: 'I love you, Helene.' Saying it at this point would, he was prepared to bet, be richly rewarded in the near future, and at worst could do no harm. It was true, too.

She put her arms round him and pulled his head on to her bosom for a moment. Then she started violently and stepped away from him. Following her eyes he saw a being resembling a four-foot-high Zulu in T-shirt and jeans apparently watching them through the window. 'Christ,' Roger said.

'It's Jimmy Fraschini,' she said, smiling and waving. The figure waved back, turned and ran off at great speed. 'Got his mask on already. The rest of them'll be by soon.' She took Roger by the forearms and stood close to him, something she rarely went out of her way to do. After a moment she said slowly: 'You know, Roger, if only you could just be a little . . .'

'Less troublesome? Less persistent? Slimmer? Younger?'

'No, just not so . . . angry. It scares me half to death, honestly. And you were quite wrong about today. I just didn't think . . .'

Judging her excuses beneath his attention, Roger thought first of how characteristic it was that this afternoon's defeat had been brought about by an alliance of Arthur and the U.S.A., then debated policy. One point must be made immediately. But as he opened his mouth to make it Helene finished speaking and without any pause turned a switch on one of the smaller devices of the kitchen. A loud moaning whine arose, unsuitable as accompaniment to talk of any dignity. It went on for some time. Before it died away, car noises and the pattering of sub-standard-sized feet, punctuated by the slam of the front-door screen, let Roger know that something wicked was coming his way. Fury made him feel temporarily several stone lighter when he looked at his watch: 4.0 exactly. He took up an offensive position near the refrigerator.

CHAPTER VI

A LITTLE BOY, or something closely resembling one, ran into the room. He wore a zip-up jacket with a big loose collar and other garments suitable to a youth twice his age, if to any human creature. His close crew-cut gave him a look of juvenile frivolity that did not match the rather florid, patrician dignity of his face. In an accent more American than Roger would have believed possible Arthur —for it was he—said to him: 'Did the prairie dog come?'

'Not yet, honey; maybe tomorrow,' Helene said, taking the question as meant for her. 'Now say hallo to Mr. Micheldene—you remember him, don't you?'

'Yes,' Arthur said ruminatively, 'I remember him.'

'Hallo, Arthur, how are you? You're quite a bit bigger than when I—'

'Is Daddy around?'

'He went over to college but he'll be home soon.'

'Has he been here long?'

'Mr. Micheldene just dropped by because he had to pay a call on a famous writer who lives near town.'

'Uh-huh. Can I have a milk shake?'

'Sure, and I've done you a turkey sandwich. Will that hold you for now?'

'Guess so. Is he staying here?'

'Don't say *he* like that, honey. Mr. Micheldene's staying in New York. He just came in to visit. Now why don't you go dress up and put your mask on and get all ready, huh?'

Looking at his mother and away from Roger for the first time, Arthur asked: 'Is there a hurry?'

'Why, no, dear, but you want to be all set when your
friends start coming by, don't you?'

'I'll finish my sandwich first.'

'Go ahead.'

Arthur sat down at the kitchen table and ate his sandwich
with peculiar ferocity, his mouth lunging at it with swift recurrent bites, then chewing with a rotary movement. He was
not closely scrutinising Roger now, just watching him.
Helene, her back to them, was busy making some spread
or whip or paste stuff. Roger decided he should say something to Arthur, but not what he felt like saying. Once,
when Arthur fired his cap-pistol a foot behind his head,
and another time, when a half-eaten toffee turned up in
the lamb's-wool lining of a glove of his, Roger had said
things to and about Arthur that might have struck Helene
as evidence of impatience or even dislike. Here was a good
chance to remove that impression, if it existed. After some
thought, Roger said:

'Did you have a nice time at school today, Arthur?'

Arthur spent some time considering this, less to prepare
an answer, it struck Roger, than to analyse in his learned
father's manner the phonetic or syntactical structure of the
question. Finally he said: 'Yeah, okay.'

'What lessons did you have?'

'Oh, all sorts.'

'Such as?'

'Excuse me?'

'Did you have arithmetic?'

'No.'

Most of Arthur's day was still unaccounted for when,
his sandwich finally despatched, he leant forward and
said: 'Would you play me at scrabble?'

Before Roger could draw in his breath Helene broke in:
'Would you, Roger? I have to wash my hair and get
ready and I shan't have a chance later.'

And so it came about that Roger found himself sitting opposite Arthur in the main room. Between them stood a cobbler's bench, an object with many useless drawers and compartments and a circular leather panel where some long-dead last-wielder had reposed his buttocks. Here the scrabble-board was set and play began.

'I should have thought you'd have been too excited to play this now, Arthur,' Roger said with a smile.

'Why should I be?'

'Well, all these letters to sort out into words and get scores, it's rather tricky, isn't it? Needs thought and so on.'

'Yeah, I know. But why should I be excited?'

'Well, aren't you and all your friends going to dress up and put on masks and . . . have a party?'

'Uh-huh.'

'Well...'

'I'm not excited,' Arthur said.

AEEEOUU was Roger's first draw from the bag. After ten minutes it had changed to AGHIIOU and Arthur, ploughing steadily on with BLUE and HOME and SEND, was well ahead. Roger began wanting very much to go away from where he was, but that point of his was still unmade and he also wanted, if possible, to get in a crafty telephone call before leaving. He put down AI on the D of SEND, scoring four points. 'That makes you twenty-nine and me sixty-four,' Arthur said with no emotion. Roger drew another H and another A.

A further set of car noises brought the prospect of relief, but the new arrival did not appear for a minute or two. Then a sudden feral howl from the doorway drew his attention. A creature with flattened humanoid features and bulging red orbs where the eyes should be advanced on him with a sleepwalker's gait. 'Blind man-eating monster from Mars,' it said in familiar thick tones.

When Arthur, laughing with horrid abandon, had run

up and been embraced, Ernst removed the silk stocking from his head and offered for inspection the crab-apples he had used for eyes. He greeted Roger with enthusiasm and asked him casually what had brought him over their way. Roger told his prepared lie about lunching with a leading novelist in the neighbourhood. Ernst barely listened. He had no curiosity about others' lives, a handy characteristic when Roger turned up in Copenhagen for a week or so at a time and explained that he was on his way to West Berlin or Athens. Helene reappeared with towel and hairbrush. Defending himself against the possible charge of having picked up a bad American habit, Ernst suggested a drink. The humiliation of being routed at scrabble by a seven-year-old seemed destined to pass Roger by.

'Oh, anything will do,' he said in answer to Ernst's question. 'You know I don't care what I drink. A little whisky, perhaps, if you have it. Water but no ice.' He started abstractedly getting to his feet.

'Hey, we're playing scrabble, remember?' Arthur said.

'Oh, I resign,' Roger said good-humouredly. 'You've won.'

'You can't resign. You have to play right through. Doesn't he, Daddy, Mommy?'

Both Ernst and Helene looked as if they supported their son.

'Oh, very well.'

'You must be strengthened in your ordeal, Roger,' Ernst said, and went off to the kitchen. Helene stayed where she was and brushed her hair.

Looking incuriously at the board, Roger saw that Arthur had put down NITER. 'Niter? What's that supposed to mean?'

'You know, like a one-nighter.'

'No such word.'

'Challenge me?'

'Most certainly I challenge you.'

'All right.' Arthur opened what was evidently a dictionary and soon said: 'Here we are. Niter. Potassium nitrate. A supposed nitrous element—'

'Rubbish, that's n, i, t, r, e.'

'Mm-mm.' Arthur shook his gleaming head. 'See for yourself.'

'I . . . But this is a bloody American dictionary.'

'This is bloody America.'

'None of that, please, Arthur,' Helene said. She had stopped brushing her hair.

'Unsuccessful challenge,' Arthur murmured, picking up the lid of the box where the rules were printed.

'But . . . that's not what you thought it meant.'

'There's nothing in the rules that says you have to know what your word means. Unsuccessful challenge: 50 points deducted from challenger's score. That makes you . . . minus 21, Mr. Micheldene.'

Helene laughed.

Roger got up so suddenly that his knee caught the edge of the board and sent the letters flying. 'Oh, I'm sorry. How frightfully clumsy of me.'

'Clumsy nothing. You did it on purpose. You saw him, didn't you, Mom? He did it on purpose, didn't he, Mommy?'

'I don't know,' Helene said. 'I wasn't watching.'

'Anyway, I'm afraid that means the end of the game.'

'It does not. I can remember where everything was.'

'I think Mr. Micheldene's probably had enough, Arthur.'

'Okay, okay, okay,' Arthur growled. 'I'm going to go dress up.'

I know a little man whose favourite toy is going to disappear suddenly soon, Roger thought to himself as Arthur swung out of the room. Helene's glance was weary. Cocking an ear for Ernst, Roger heard the refrigerator door

slam. He said with a smile: 'Terrifyingly bright, that off-
spring of yours.'

'Yeah.'

'Budding genius.' Then he said in a gentle, or at any
rate quiet, voice: 'Helene dear.'

'Yeah?'

He had never felt timid or hesitant in his life, but did
his best with blinking, lip-licking and just not speaking yet.
Finally he quavered: 'The weekend. You will arrange
something then, won't you?'

She looked away quickly, then back at him. 'I'll try.'

'Not just try, darling. Please.'

'Roger, all I can do is try, can't you see? It doesn't just
depend on me. All sorts of other people'll be around and
I'll have things to see to. But really I'll do what I can to
fix it. I really will.'

At this evasion a part of Roger—one of which the rest
of him on the whole disapproved—wanted to step forward
and give Helene a medium-weight slap across the chops.
But all of him was easily sensitive and intelligent enough
to realise that that kind of treatment would undoubtedly
worsen rather than improve his chances of satisfaction at
the weekend. So he followed a radically different line
whereby affable balding Roger, popular quirky Roger,
urbane much-travelled Roger took over from noted alco-
holist Roger, esurient Roger, famed goat-getter and dirt-
doer Roger. Quipped he to handsome hospitable word-
pundit Dr. Ernst Bang, 32: 'Oh, thanks.'

He kept it up in the intervals of being introduced to
Paul and Mary Selby and young Jay Selby and George
and Evelyn Fraschini and Jimmy Fraschini and Karen
Fraschini and Martha Selby and Bob and Ann Sullivan and
Clay and Sue Green and Russ Green and George Fraschini
Jr. There were others whose names he never heard but
who, in the forms of miniature spacemen, witches, Red

Indians, goblins and Frankenstein's monsters, burst in and snatched up the packets Helene had prepared and ate what was in them and ran about shouting. At a climax of this Roger asked to use the telephone and went into the kitchen.

Soon a voice was saying into his ear: 'Miranda, good-afternoon.'

'May I speak to Mrs. Atkins, please?'

'Who's calling, please?'

'George Green here.'

'One moment, Mr. Green.'

Almost at once another voice said: 'Mollie Atkins speaking.'

Good, Roger thought, but still could not visualise the face that went with the voice. 'This isn't George Green, this is Roger Micheldene.'

'Hi, hallo, how are you?'

'Surviving. Look, are you free at all this evening?'

'Well no, I'm afraid not. We have a dinner party and I have to get home right away and start things going. You could come to dinner if you want.'

'Oh. Yes, I might, I suppose.'

'On the other hand Strode'll be there and you two didn't seem to get along too well the last time you met, I remember thinking.'

'No, there is that. Well . . .'

'Listen, why don't you come and see me tomorrow afternoon? I'm free then. I could take you on a little scenic drive.'

'All right. What time?'

'Come around at three.'

'What, to this . . . shop of yours?'

'Sure, why not? You'll just love it. You'll be coming by train? All right, there's one gets in at six minutes of three. You take that one, old boy.'

Roger said he would, rang off, made two more calls and

went back to where the people and children were. The people were taking notice of the children in that curious American way, talking to them, picking them up, even running about with them. A man asked Roger if he had any children and Roger said no and the man evidently saw that he had been put in his place and said nothing more. Then another man—either George Fraschini or Clay Green, or possibly Paul Selby—said he hoped very much that Roger would be able to manage to come along and have dinner with everybody when the party moved to his place.

'So kind of you,' Roger said, taking a pinch of Golden Cardinal from his pewter snuff-box, 'but I must be getting back to New York very soon.'

There was a general gasp of astonishment, incredulity and protest, as if Roger had announced that he expected the Federal authorities to deport him next morning. Those who had not heard what he said came hurrying anxiously over to be informed. 'But he can't go. Look what it'll do to his evening. It's out of the question. When will he eat? Evelyn, you tell him. Anyway, there's no train. Ernst, do you have a schedule? Give him another drink, quick. I'll drive him back.'

Roger found this reaction agreeable rather than the opposite. Helene, he saw, was standing at a window, hold-ing in her arms a small child of uncertain sex with whom she was apparently discussing the view. The child's hand rested lightly on the back of her neck. Roger said: 'No, I'm afraid I really must be going. And don't worry about the train—there's one from that junction place in about half an hour. I've ordered a taxi.'

There was more objection, centring on how far away the junction was and how huge the taxi fare would be and he must let Bob-Paul-George drive him, but it had died down into dissident muttering by the time the taxi came and Roger, waving Helene good-bye, went and got into it. Before it had moved more than a couple of yards another car turned off the road into the Bangs' drive. Roger fancied he could hear laughter from it. When it stopped Irving Macher and Suzanne Klein and Nigel Pargeter, strongly illuminated in the porch light, got out and moved in an undisciplined manner towards the front door. Although now being carried away from this scene at an accelerating twenty miles an hour, Roger pressed himself well back against the cushions.

'You're missing out on a lot of fun, aren't you, travelling at this time?' the driver asked.

'If you don't mind terribly I prefer not to talk.'

'Anything you say.'

On either side of the road were houses festooned with multi-coloured lights and orange-coloured turnip ghosts. Now and again ragged groups of people or children could be seen cavorting about. What did they think they were celebrating?

The distance of the houses from one another, their wooden construction, the absence of horticulture and fences or walls, the woodland setting, all combined to give the area the look of a semi-temporary encampment for a battalion of parvenus. Not a bad image of America as a whole, eh?

Roger met an alternative image when the taxi got on to one of those throughway or turnpike things. It was a great charade of light and sound and movement aimed at the participants themselves. By having so many tons of metal hurtling along at these speeds, you see, hooting, winking, overtaking, they hoped to convince themselves and one another that they had energy and were important and were going somewhere. Nevertheless it was being done in remarkable quantity and with some conviction. As the taxi accelerated past a line of large trailer-lorries got up with strings of lights like the houses he had just seen, and two five-yard-wide cars with a dozen rear lights apiece swept by him in turn in the left-hand lane, he found it surprisingly difficult to feel absolutely sure that he had not spent his whole life travelling down this turnpike, that anything anywhere else existed, that Helene existed. It was as if the whole effort of all these furious lumps of matter had its point in separating him and her as decisively as possible. He was quite relieved when he saw the pale blue lights of an exit ahead and his driver pulled over to the right and began to slow down.

CHAPTER VII

Roger was not feeling very well when he came out of the station at Ammanford, Pa. and went in search of Miranda. The train, though fast and not barbarously uncomfortable, had been full of Americans. He had chosen his railway reading badly. And what he drank and ate in the bar car had not been good for his stomach. That organ was still striving to normalise itself after last night's intake of a lot of things called French 75s. (Half an hour with the telephone and not really very much effrontery had finally got him to a party somewhere in Greenwich Village. Two of the three presentable girls at it had each been accompanied throughout by a separate bearded Australian painter talking about artistic integrity; the third had pleaded lesbianism.) Not caring what one drank unfortunately did not guarantee not caring what one had drunk. He wished he could recapitulate now some parts of the brief but varied belching recital he had given in the taxi from his hotel to Pennsylvania Station. No good, though.

The reading-matter business had been worse really. He ought to have remembered that the *New York Times* lived by the assumption that everybody needed to know everything about everything. Information doled out in sheer quantity—as might be expected. They should stick to what they were good at or at any rate had made their own— *Time, Life* and so on—instead of trying to ape the London *Times*. And then—worse yet—there was *Blinkie Heaven*. There had seemed no danger at all in bringing this along to

share with the *New York Times* the task of distracting him
from having to look out of the window (and from the atten-
dant risks of noticing something of what was to be seen out
there). His recent injunction to the Author of all things to
see to it that this particular one of his works should turn
out strikingly below par had been, he had fancied at the
time, almost a matter of form, an agreeable courtesy
whereby one said please for what was coming one's way
anyhow—like ordering a drink. Reading the first couple of
chapters of Macher's stuff had caused Roger several emotions, the most painful of which had been that of a man
who finds that, quite out of the blue, he has not been given
this day his daily bread.

It was not that the thing was a *good* novel. Macher's
nationality, and existence in the present century, guaranteed that. Even before *Clarissa* there had only been a few
touches in Aphra Behn and Defoe (*Colonel Jack*, of course,
not *Crusoe* or *Moll Flanders*), and what was there since?
No, the sorry-no-daily-bread sign had been hung out when
Roger saw that if his firm did not take it a dozen others
would leap at it, and that it would be a success. He could
have written out the follow-up advertisement there and
then. 'A profoundly disturbing and yet deeply compas-
sionate vision of the human situation'—Philip Toynbee.
'Perhaps one of the four most poised and authoritative con-
tributions of the New York neo-Gothic meta-fantasy school'
—*Times Literary Supplement*. 'This searing, sizzling,
lacerating I.C.B.M. of a book will pick you up, throw you
down and trample on you—*Daily Express*. 'Remarkable'—
Yorkshire Post.

It was tempting to turn it down notwithstanding and say
in due course that there were some successes which a house
of any integrity ought to be proud not to have published.
That sort of stuff went down well as a rule in Roger's firm.
With a staff of readers as dead as theirs to even the most

blatant selling quality, it had to. But Roger had recently
rather weakened his authority as champion of art vs. profit
by successfully fighting for the rejection of a first novel
by a young West Indian on the grounds that it was *in love
with evil*. Appearing soon afterwards under a rival imprint,
the book had not only sold half a million copies in the first
six months, been accepted for translation into all Europe's
major tongues with Japanese thrown in and broken a
record or two with the sum paid for its film rights, but had
won two international awards and unprovoked commenda-
tions from Sartre, Moravia and Graham Greene. None of
this might have mattered but for the widespread feeling
that the book had encountered early opposition less because
it was in love with evil than because its author was very
much not in love with Roger and even more so the other
way round. A well-attended party in Maida Vale had been
the scene of flat disagreement between black man and
white man on the subject of the future of Africa's new
nations. Negro arguments had been effectively silenced
when an Anglo-Saxon head (Roger's) butted their pro-
ponent in the stomach.

What was in one way most galling to Roger about
Blinkie Heaven was that it was not, as he had first suspected, entirely staffed by the kind of character America
had made its primary fictional concern. There were blind
people, true, and the odd Negro, but they were not backed
up by the expected paraplegic necrophiles, hippoerotic
jockeys, exhibitionistic castrates, coprophagic pig-farmers,
armless flagellationists and the rest of the bunch. People like
shopkeepers, pedestrians, New Englanders, neighbours,
graduates, uncles walked Macher's pages. Events took place
and the reader could determine what they were. There was
spoken dialogue, appearing between quotation marks.
Never mind: as Roger approached Miranda he was con-
soling himself with the thought of what acceptance by his

firm would mean for this particular fiction in prose. Stinginess over advertising space and with proof copies, caution about the size of the first impression would ensure a sale at least 10,000 fewer than most rivals could manage. But why, oh why, he questioned the All-Merciful, must he fall back on that?

Miranda turned out to be a small double-fronted shop between a delicatessen and a booze emporium. That was all right as far as it went. He peered in past racks of hairy neckties and asymmetrical stands of shoes and sandals too ugly not to be hand-made. Glass and pottery rejects of various sizes and uncertain function stood on triangular shelves. Here and there on the rush mats that covered parts of the floor were groups of wrought-iron vessels in which the very industrious or the very apathetic might one day boil water or even make a soup. Although the day was overcast, the green and white sunblinds had been lowered and visibility inside was poor. Nevertheless, several unmistakable women could be made out in the distance.

Roger crossed Miranda's threshold decisively, confident that Caliban, or perhaps better Stephano, was if not driving hard in his New York office then at any rate drunkenly asleep there. A girl of Oriental appearance, who would have been quite acceptable if she had had eye-sockets as well as eyes, came forward and said: 'Good-afternoon, sir, and what can I show you this afternoon?'

Although relieved at not having to start on the wantee-speakee-missee drill he had been contemplating, Roger would have preferred something less impeccably American. However, he replied at once in what he thought of as a cool brisk tone: 'Oh, good-afternoon to you. I wonder if I could possibly have a word with Mrs. Atkins. Would you kindly let her know that Mr. Micheldene is here, please?'

The girl looked him up and down for about a second and a half before saying: 'Sure, I'll kindly let her know.

One moment, please.' Her earlier friendliness had largely abated. She looked again and went away.

Roger recognised this treatment. They thought that because you spoke like an Englishman you must be homosexual, which only testified to their deep doubts of their own masculinity. It was true that this girl was a girl, not a man, but the principle held.

A middle-aged Negro woman, six feet tall and pretty near as close to jet black as the human skin can get, pushed her way through a bead curtain and came towards him. His mouth opened a short distance. Surely . . . No, rubbish, of course not. Actually this sort of thing was proving a great help : race and colour as an unexpected extra variable to eke out his small stock of Mollie Atkins recognition-aids. Given a few Red Indians and Indians and a Bushman or two as the others present in the shop, he was sure of being easily able to pick out Mollie Atkins, about whom all he knew for certain at the moment was that she stood between 4 ft. 6 ins. and 6 ft. 6 ins. and was in the 25-55 age-group.

The coloured woman picked up a large potted plant with leaves like starched leather and carried it back towards the curtained aperture, through which there now appeared another female, of unmistakably Caucasian stock this time. Roger blinked and screwed up his eyes convulsively a few times to provide evidence of short sight if necessary. Even while doing this he could see enough of the Caucasian female to make him invoke the Prince of Peace (*secreto*, or nearly) and wonder briefly how many gin and tonics he must have put down that evening at Joe Derlanger's place.

Then they were face to face. At this range she looked a little better, but not much. A complexion that appeared to have been left out in a violent hailstorm for about ten years was her most signal drawback. There were others. However, she stood an excellent chance of being Mollie Atkins, and if she was she had one great overriding virtue.

The smile she gave him was cordial enough, though tinged with just a little more inquiry, he thought, than fitted someone who knew who he was. He gave a much better smile back, with more eye-work and a quiet hallo. This, born of long practice, was aimed at alleviating that continuous trouble over names and faces which besets sufferers from alcoholic amnesia. It could be taken either as a token of tremendous intimacy or as the routine greeting of a very nice, but not necessarily very heterosexual, man.

Anyway, it then became magically all right. Mollie Atkins declared herself sufficiently unmistakably as such by saying emphatically : 'Hi.'

Roger did not really like this vocable, but recognised its role. 'Very good to see you,' he said, packing sincerity in.

'I thought we might take off.'

'That sounds like a perfectly splendid idea.'

'Where would you like to go ?'

'Oh, anywhere, really.'

'What sort of place ?'

'I leave it to you.'

'I thought somewhere quiet.'

'So did I.'

'If Miss Hartogensis calls tell her it'll be there tomorrow afternoon,' Mollie said, but evidently not to Roger. The Japanese girl (what made her think she could ever pass unnoticed in a white man's world, however hard she worked at her accent?) smiled and nodded in a submissive fashion. At this Roger experienced a sensation of strong approval and reassurance. There were obviously still quite a few white people about in the Administration and in allied spheres, probably enough to see him and other American clients out.

With no more said, Roger found himself outside. A large white car, with its name or some equally inflammatory slogan written more than once on it in gold script, was parked nearby. He got into it and prepared to be driven away. It was one of his boasts that he never drove and saw no need to learn. Like dancing. As well as putting other men into the implied position of having to work like hell at ancillary skills in order just to stay level in the social and sexual race, this non-qualification of his could have more direct benefits. To make him feel that the universe was indeed ruled by and through a divinely appointed hierarchy (a decreasingly common experience of late), few experiences had ever worked better than an encounter featuring himself, a stockbroker's wife who was much too proud of her lilac-and-cream Mercedes, and a policeman. The last-named had put his head into the bar they were having a quickie in and said: 'Driver of car 923 DUW please,' and Roger had smiled winsomely and said: 'That's you, isn't it, sweetheart?' before turning away and asking the barmaid, a girl with protruding teeth but memorable as the owner of the furthest-apart breasts he had ever seen, whether she would care to join him in a little gargle.

Mollie Atkins—if this woman was actually somebody else altogether it seemed to be making no great difference—said as she moved the car into thin traffic: 'How's my old friend Helene Bang?'

Annoyance visited Roger, slightly less at the content of this question than at its timing. Answering it, or rather meeting it with a properly vituperative counter-question, belonged far better to the period after, rather than before, the act he hoped to be performing in the near future. He said as lightly as he could manage: 'Very well, as far as I know.'

'That far's fairly far, isn't it?'

He brought his head round towards her an inch at a time. 'I'm afraid I don't altogether . . .'

'Understand? I'll have to see if I can't put it more plainly. I don't know whether you've been to bed with

Helene or not but you obviously want to very much **and**
as long as you do want to you'll keep trying, being you. **I**
was just asking how you've been making out recently.'

'I fail to see how—'

'Now quit this fail to see bit, old boy. If you really **can't**
see then *try harder*. I want to know where I stand **with**
you, that's all. I think that's normal and reasonable. I know
a lot already, believe me, but there's a little more I'd **like**
to know. Are you with me so far?'

'So far, yes.' Roger glanced coldly out of the window **but**
his eye fell at once on a building that looked like **selections**
from a concrete battleship, with masts and turrets and **port-**
holes. It had a chromium cross stuck on its maintop **to**
denote its function. So he glanced back in again.

'Are you in love with the fair Helene?'

He said immediately : 'Yes. Very much. I have **been**
for years.' Without being strikingly bold this was a good,
sound piece of play. So far from resenting an avowal **of**
love directed elsewhere, they positively welcomed it (**unless**
of course they were beginning to consider themselves **candi-**
dates for such an avowal, which was not going to **happen**
here). It was as if they thought even a mortgaged heart **was**
better than none.

'Any ambitions? Long-term, I mean?'

He shrugged his shoulders and tried to look dejected.
'Oh, quite hopeless,' he said, which was dictated by **security**
considerations as well as being tactically correct.

'So I should imagine. I think you'd probably have **to**
wait for—what's he called? Ernst?—to die, wouldn't **you?**
And that's going to take longer than you can afford. **You**
married?'

'Legally, yes.'

'Well, as to that one that's all I need to know for **now.**
And you go back to Europe when?'

'I leave for England on Tuesday week.'

'Twelve days. Oh well. We should last nicely. It's a bit of a trip for you to make, though, all this way down here by rail. Don't you drive?'

'I've never learnt.'

'No, I guess you never did. Maybe I'd better come up to New York some time to do a little shopping. About a half-hour's shopping. Do you have an apartment?'

'I'm living in a flat that belongs to a friend of mine who's away, but his son's in and out of the place all the time and I can hardly bar the door on him.'

'You can't? I'd have thought that was just the type of stuff you'd be good at. Why can't you bar the door on him?'

'Well, for one thing unless I literally did that he'd probably come barging in regardless, and as likely as not with half a dozen chums. He doesn't hold on to much of what you say to him. He's nearly always frightfully tight, you see. And the way it often takes him, if I did really bolt the door he's perfectly capable of smashing it down.'

'How old is this kid?'

'Oh, early twenties, I imagine.'

'The young learn fast these days, don't they? Well, I can see it might be difficult. I could probably fix something myself. We have this apartment of our own and Strode hardly ever uses it but I never know when he might. Anyhow, we can talk about that later. By the way, next time you come down here I may be able to find us somewhere indoors. It won't be easy but I'll try. We ought to be all right today, though. It's a pity there isn't any sun but the air's still quite warm. Would you mind giving me a hand with this junk?'

The junk consisted of a blanket, two pillows, and a wicker hamper. Mollie handed it out to Roger from the back of the now stationary car, then looked up in the direction of a large white house fifty yards away and on the far side of the land where they had stopped. 'I don't suppose those people would mind if we parked here for a spell, do you?' she muttered.

'Why, they don't usually, do they?'

She laughed a lot, showing rather good teeth, though not as good as Helene's. 'Holmes, this is amazing. How did you guess?'

'Nothing to it, my dear. Just the way you drove straight to this exact spot—the nearest suitable one, I presume. How long did it take us, five minutes? No more.'

'Four and half from the shop is regular for the course. When I'm in love I can clip it back to a little over four. It's nice it's so handy. Yes sir, there's quite a deal of wide open spaces still around in this man's country.'

'Do you come here often?' Roger asked as, with a thick belt of trees and bushes between them and the road, they came to a small clearing and spread the blanket on top of fallen leaves and thin grass.

'Not as often as I'd like, but still pretty often. I have this knack of making friends easily, you see, and a surprising number of them keep coming around between girl friends or when their wives go visiting their folks. Is the boss acting up? Do your teenage kids and their buddies make the house uninhabitable? Nothing on television worth a damn? Call up old trouble-free punctual Mollie and you'll get that same Southern welcome whether you've been away a day or ten years. Oh, it's really lovely here in the summer and so safe. You could hear people coming a long time before they could see you but there's never anyone around. You can just relax and enjoy yourself.'

While she talked she had been unpacking the hamper. Next to her as she sat on the blanket there now lay a bottle of gin, a bottle of dry vermouth, a wooden ice-bucket with a copper lid, a slender glass jug, a glass stirring-rod and two glasses. 'Which would you like to try first?' she asked.

'I think I'll start with some of that,' Roger said, pointing at her.

He had some of that. It was really quite good, well matured but showing no untoward signs of age and with the consumer's satisfaction borne very much in mind. The trouble was the talking. It ran in part:

'Oh yes. Oh, it's great, it's so great, it's wonderful. Oh, yes, yes. Oh, you're so strong, so fine, so good, so good for me. Oh, what you do to me, darling. Oh, it's so great. Oh, yes.'

He was not tempted to laugh—that had never been one of his troubles. Even when he glanced up and saw a tortoise under a fern a yard away watching them he kept a resolutely straight face. No: what this vocal accompaniment did was to distract him from that total absorption in his own sensations which he required from what he was now doing. He remembered for the first time that it had been the same down by the Derlangers' swimming-pool. But, sensing that this was not the stage at which to tell the lady to belt up, he saw it through in grim silence to the end.

'Would you like some of this now?' Mollie asked, dropping ice-cubes into the jug.

'Oh, thanks most awfully. Not too dry for me, if I may.'

She gazed at him as she stirred the drink and what must once have been a pair of dimples showed when she grinned. 'Rog, old boy,' she said, 'I hate to say it, but you certainly are one fat Englishman. It was like fighting a grizzly bear. Not that I'm objecting, you understand. Just mentioning it as an interesting fact.'

Roger said crossly: 'Yes yes, that's all very well, but what about that tortoise that was hanging round here a minute ago? Look, there it is now. It is a tortoise, I suppose, is it? What's it doing here, anyway? Is it someone's pet or what? Good God, there's another one. What's going on?'

'Oh, there are a lot of them around here. They just live here, I guess. They're wild.'

'I dare say they are,' Roger went on, not appeased in the slightest, 'but I'm by no means sure they're tortoises at all. Black shell with yellow patches—I've never heard of a tortoise like that. No, that's not a true tortoise. Must be some kind of—'

'They're called turtles,' Molly said mildly.

'Well, whatever they may or may not be they're clearly not that. A turtle lives in the sea and has sort of flipper things instead of proper feet. Quite a different kettle of fish.'

Roger accepted his drink without a word and brooded a moment. He was still nettled at the way these tortoises, or tortoise-like creatures, had been obtruded upon his environment, illegitimately foisted in.

'I could find out all about them from somebody,' Mollie said, 'if it means that much to you.'

'If two of them go by here within a couple of minutes of each other, then the wood must be absolutely crawling with the damn things. I seem to remember reading some-where that dogs eat tortoises. Well, you'd have thought—'

'I can see they're eating at you, these turtles or tortoises or whatever they are. What would you have liked to happen?'

'I don't follow you, I'm afraid.'

'Wait, I believe I know what it is. You think Washington ought to have consulted you before allowing packs of savage tortoises to roam around at will. In fact, though, I hear they're pretty harmless, despite their formidable appearance. Never been known to attack man.'

'Please try not to talk tripe.'

'Well, don't blame me, old boy, I didn't bring them here.

They just rolled along of their own free will. Anyway, can we get off tortoises now for a while? Drink that down and let me pour you another.'

Roger submitted. He was still dissatisfied with the tortoise situation but there was obviously no advantage in prolonging the discussion. Nevertheless it had put him a couple of points down conversationally and this must be redressed at once. 'How's my old friend Strode?' he asked.

'Now there I'm in the very fortunate position of complete and unassailable ignorance. I don't have the remotest idea of how your old friend Strode is, I have no way of knowing and I'm not about to try to accumulate any information on the subject. I told you I like to know roughly where I stand with people in this sort of situation. I also like to let them know where they stand. Which includes telling them how I feel about my husband. When I first really got to find out what he was like, after we'd been married about six months, I hated him. Now that we've been married fourteen years and I have a much larger stock of information at my disposal, I hate him. There has been some change in my feelings, though. As of the last five or six years I also consider he's a jerk.'

Roger was as little pleased with the turn the chat had taken as he had been when worsted over the tortoises. He said coldly: 'It sounds as if you've a strong case for leaving him.'

'Oh yes, very. But a slightly stronger case for staying around. I need to use money and I have no money and I have no trade or skill and nobody else has ever wanted to marry me.'

'What about that shop affair of yours?'

'Are you kidding? In a good year Miranda loses five thousand dollars. I'd think anybody who knew anything about money could see that as soon as he set eyes on it.

Strode's what one would call good about this. You probably think Miranda's nonsense but I don't. I get a big bang out of having all that stuff around and showing it to people and having them like it. I wouldn't want not to have this. So I stay with Strode. He doesn't notice how I feel about him. Or about anything else. Everybody he knows, everything he does, his whole life, you see, it's all just a thing he does himself. What he's not doing doesn't exist.'

It was time, Roger considered, to restore perspectives. 'Sounds to me like an old-fashioned case of egotism,' he said in a dismissive tone. 'There are plenty of—'

'Sure, but even egotists like to make an effect on people, have them admire them or be afraid of them or something like this. Strode's a stage further in. It isn't even that he doesn't care. He doesn't notice.'

After not listening to rather a lot more of the same, Roger jack-knifed himself a good deal nearer on heels and buttocks, then did his smile with eye-crinkle. 'Aren't we talking rather a lot?' he asked.

She looked away and patted her fringe. 'I guess we are, I'm sorry. I should have told you you only get this the first time around. From here on in it's strictly art movies and the World Series and moon shots, I promise. I'm sorry, Roger. Drink up now. Oh . . .' She smiled suddenly and reached across to the hamper. 'I almost forgot. I got this for you. I hope you like it.'

It was one of the fat fifty-cent horrors made of equal parts of Java reject and sawdust. 'What made you think of that?' he asked curiously.

'Just at the Derlangers' I noticed you seemed to go for cigars, cutting the end in a special way and all. Is it the right kind?'

Of the recognised procedures for dealing with unacceptable cigars Roger rejected his favourite, that of saying he hoped nobody would mind terribly if he cut it up and smoked it in his pipe. He was about to adopt the alternative and thrust the thing into his jacket pocket with a force obviously more than enough to fracture it. And then he found himself laying it carefully down at the edge of the blanket and saying: 'Do you mind if I leave it till later?'

'Take your own time, sir.'

He could not remember at all clearly now just how bad the talking had been before they had their first drink. If it was really bad in future he would tell her—afterwards, naturally—not to do it any more. But this might well entail tact and patience, an unfavourable sign at such an early stage. He congratulated himself on his foresight in constructing that dipsomaniacal son for the friend who was putting him up in New York. Letting them enter one's base of operations was to be avoided whenever possible. And if the occasion did arise urgently he could always dismantle the son, send him to an alcoholics' institution, draft him into the Navy, hospitalise him after a brawl.

'I'd like some more of that now,' he said.

CHAPTER VIII

'THIS IS FATHER COLGATE.'

Oh, what nonsense, how can it be? was Roger's thought as a flamboyantly handsome and muscular man of thirty, dressed up for some unfathomable reason of his own in strict but well-tailored clerical garb, shook his hand and told him he was very glad to know him. And how could he know him after five seconds' acquaintance? Still, by the same token Roger could not very well accuse the fellow immediately of masquerading, and until he knew more he decided to follow his usual policy towards actual priests, a show of cordial respect and interest. The normal response to a few minutes of this was the query whether Roger himself was not of the faith. Roger would say yes, with the silent qualification that he was of the faith chiefly in the sense that the church he currently did not attend was Catholic, and would go on to be fairly daring and original about Arianism. It was intrinsically worth while to be seen to be in with the priesthood, as well as going down well with the women he always saw to it were about. Even so, he could not help leaning sarcastically on the last word when he now asked: 'Are your duties connected with the College, Father?'

'No, they are not,' the man replied with a touch of impatience, as if rebuking some wearisomely common doctrinal confusion. 'Budweiser is a Protestant foundation, as might be expected in this part of the country. There was no substantial number of communicants here until ten or fifteen years ago.'

'And now?'

'Pardon me?'

'The number of communicants nowadays?'

'Substantial,' the supposed divine said, and inhaled his cigarette in such a way as to cause a ball of smoke to come into being for an instant above the back of his tongue before vanishing with a hiss. 'Substantial,' he added, nodding.

'Oh, how frightfully agreeable.'

'Yes, right now there's plenty of God's grace around in these parts.'

This was unsatisfactory. Even an impersonator should be able to do better. 'Do you really think so?' Roger asked incredulously.

'These are happy people. Certainly they have their problems—who doesn't?—but they do their best to help one another with them and they have charity. If that's not a heavenly gift I'd like to know what is. Are you yourself of any religious communion, sir?'

Now this, again, had come too soon to be altogether welcome. 'It so happens that I am—of the Roman Catholic Church, actually.'

'Uh-huh.' The ecclesiastic showed no interest or even evidence of recognition, let alone pleasure. Perhaps he belonged to some appalling sort of local High Anglican thing. Just as likely he had been christened Father, did football-stadium revivalism and enjoyed dressing up. Well, as far as the last part went he would be squarely in the line of Church tradition. One of Roger's chronic difficulties was reconciling his belief in the importance of priests and the Church with his antipathy towards most of the former and aversion from most of the doctrines and practices of the latter, a conflict also to be seen in his relations with the Omnipotent. Accepting a fresh drink from an anonymous hand, he tried to suppress all that for the moment and give this black-clad clown his last fair chance by listening to some of what he was saying.

There was plenty of it. Father Colgate described himself as an optimist and personally had no fault to find with such a condition, or so he said. The Deity's steady rise in grace-output over the years, he explained, stood in direct ratio to the increase, both qualitative and quantitative, in the love which human beings lavished upon their Maker whether they knew it or not. 'Ever since I attained a condition in which I was able to take stock of the evidence of this,' he went on and on and on, 'I have been more forcibly struck every day by its profusion and variety. People are kinder to one another than they were. They have forethought : they attempt to gauge in advance the probable or likely effects on those around them of the course of action they have a mind to pursue. They say to themselves, I intend to initiate a certain chain of events. What can I expect the results of this to be and what further chains of events will thereby be set in motion ?'

While Roger waited for an opening he noticed that half a dozen young men and women were gathering round the pair of them as they stood by the window of the lofty, heavily-panelled room. For sophomores or seniors or whatever the hell they were of Budweiser College, Pa., they seemed not hopelessly barbarous. None of them was chewing gum or smoking a ten-cent cigar or wearing a raccoon coat or drinking Coca-Cola or eating a hamburger or sniffing cocaine or watching television or mugging anyone or, perforce, driving a Cadillac. Quite a little minority culture group. It was true that some of them must voluntarily have joined the fraternity on whose premises and by whose hospitality he was now beginning to get drunk, but presumably they would not be here otherwise, and he wanted some sort of audience for what he was preparing to tell Father Colgate. One of their number, a blonde girl

wearing a man's shirt but in all other visible respects un-
manly to the point of outright effeminacy, was looking at
him. These Yank college girls were at it all the time, one
heard. But anything like that was going to have to wait until
after he had given his lecture and the party reassembled
here or, preferably, in somebody's private house. For the
moment he must concentrate on showing this blonde, and
any other relevant person within earshot, how marvellous
he was at dealing with chaps like Father Colgate.

That churchman had worked his way through forethought and was now on about responsibility. Both quali-
ties involved the use of reason, he said. Roger waited until
the other had finished explaining the first of two alternative
definitions of the word—a perfect breaking-in point—and
then said fast and loud:

'I honestly don't know which staggers me more, Father,
your affection for the obvious or your half-baked humani-
tarianism. To hear you talk one would imagine God to be
some sort of corporation president with strong views on
group morale and togetherness and all that tomfoolery.
Getting a good healthy creative atmosphere going. Loyalty
up and loyalty down and loyalty all round. Nailing up
those idiotic notices saying Think. One big happy family
with every member a success. Religion is what I gather you
people call a bull session—rather a good phrase in one
sense, actually. White-haired old man up on the top floor
who knows what's going on in every corner of the organisation and never too busy to listen to anybody's problems
even if all they do is sweep the floors or work the lift.
Superhuman only in scale.'

Without pausing or altering the direction of his gaze
Roger lunged with both hands at a loaded tray being
carried past by a black girl in a white dress. Of the two
drinks thus secured he held one at the ready and put the
other on a nearby shelf for not much later, continuing:

'Is your imagination so puny that the vast terror and horror
of the mystery simply passes you by altogether? Has it
never occurred to you that we're bound to God by ties of
fear and anger and resentment as well as love? And do you
know what despair is like? And what makes you think you
know anything at all about what he feels about us? I don't
say it isn't love, I don't know either, but if it is it's a pretty
odd kind of love, isn't it? Pretty odd. But I suppose one
couldn't expect you to have noticed that. No, your sensi-
bility's been packaged and air-conditioned and refrigerated
out of existence. Nobody could say you're not in touch with
the modern world, Father, I'll give you that. I rather envy
you, I must confess, with your Fifth Avenue vestments and
your commuter communicants and your neon Christ and
your hungover penitents—what do you give them, a Hail
Mary for every martini after the first three? Yes, it must
be quite fun. The only thing is, you will insist on calling
it religion. Or has that gone, too?'

A new voice now spoke. It was not very familiar to
Roger, but it was much more familiar than he wanted it
to be. It belonged to Irving Macher, who had arrived unnoticed at Roger's side. It said: 'Pretty competent, sir,
but overly scripted, wouldn't you say? A little lacking in
spontaneity?'

'What the devil are you doing here?' Roger asked in
genuine surprise.

'Well, being a member of Rho Ep and—I'm sorry, Mr.
Micheldene, you see I belong to the fraternity that owns
this house, and so when I heard you were being enter-
tained here I naturally came over to renew acquaintance.
I'd like to have you meet some of my friends.—You remember my telling you about Mr. Micheldene from England? Well, this is he.—And this is Tom Shumway, Mr.
Micheldene, and Prince Castlemaine, who runs the radio
station, and Ed Hirsch our star quarter-back—that's a

position in the kind of football we play over here, Mr.
Micheldene—and John Page and Pitt Hubler. Tell me, sir,
will you be doing us the honour of dining with us here
tonight?'

'Good God no. They told me I had the alternative of
eating at six or at six forty-five and I've roughed it a bit
in my time but I'm afraid I rather draw the line at sitting
down to a knife-and-fork tea after an hour's drinking. No
no, I'll be dining later with Professor Parrish and a few
people he wants me to meet.'

Roger was aware he was being sidetracked, physically as
well as verbally, for moving to face Macher's group had
taken him away from his previous circle of listeners, including the girl with the shirt and the man of God. Colgate
had reacted fairly satisfactorily to being told how he stood,
doing nothing beyond staring photogenically back at Roger
and shaking his head slowly and slightly from time to time.
It would have been suitable if he had tried to come back
with some feeble denial or deprecation and thus earned
a definite pulping, but by and large he had been adequately
seen off. In any case, the task now was to engineer the
punishment of Macher for his interruption.

'I know I sometimes strike you as a trifle slow on the
uptake, Mr. Macher,' Roger said, taking a pinch of
George IV from his silver snuff-box, 'but I'd like to take
you up, if I may, on what you were saying just now.
Would you care to amplify it, perhaps? Do forgive me for
liking things to be made what may seem to you excessively
clear—it's a little weakness of mine, I'm afraid.'

In Macher's shoes Roger would have countered this by
pretending to have forgotten what he had said, but Macher
said at once: 'Of course. It's not that you and I differ very
much, in our basic views, that is. Or rather—I'm not
putting this too well—some of the ideas you were pro-
pounding just now come pretty close to the way I feel. My

objection was you gave the whole thing too much production. Sounded rehearsed. And that means it probably was rehearsed. Like a lot of things you do, Mr. Micheldene, speaking with all respect. Now I don't regard it as a crime for people to be different than me; I'd say I'm at least as tolerant as you. It's just that I like people to behave naturally, without looking to the effect all the time. To me that's behaving like a human being, living by impulse. And—again you'll have to forgive my presumption—I don't think you do that often enough. You weren't really sore with that clergyman at all; you were just doing your stuff. And the sort of stuff it was Graham Greene does a whole sight better.'

Throughout this Roger had been producing his pigskin case and taking a cigar from it with what he hoped was hypnotic deliberation. Certainly everybody but Macher was watching the process. 'Are you charging me with insincerity, Mr. Macher?' Roger asked amiably.

'Certainly not, Mr. Micheldene, that would be most presumptuous of me. Not conscious insincerity, at any rate. How could I? Everything I know about the intentions behind what you say I derive from what you say. And what you say sounds to me like a performance. It's a matter of the modes of speech you favour.'

'Ah hell, Irv,' the young man perhaps called Hirsch said, 'Literary Criticism 332—less of it, for Christ's sake.'

'Do you think, Mr. Macher,' Roger said, 'that with your necessarily rather confined experience of the English language you're entitled to pontificate about . . . what was that bit of jargon? Forms of speech?'

Macher did a longer laugh than usual. 'Well, it's true I haven't had the chance of speaking any kind of language half as long as you have, sir, but with that reservation . . . As a native American in full possession of his faculties I can claim complete parity with you as a user of English. I could go a little further and just, uh, inform you that as regards the development of the language the U.S.A. is now central and England peripheral, but I don't—'

'Son of a bitch, Irv,' Hirsch said, 'Dr. Bang's linguistic preceptorial—it's as if you can't ever—'

'You mean you don't find the learned Doctor's society rewarding, Ed?' Macher asked. 'Indirectly, in any event.'

'God damn it, Irv, I didn't say that, I just meant I was getting bugged by—'

'Because I personally have no fault to find with him.' Macher looked at Roger. 'Most particularly not in regard to his taste in wives.'

All the other young men except one broke into yelping cries. 'I should say not. Some doll. Jesus, is she stacked. Oh, murder. Boy, what a piece of ass. Could I use her. Wow.'

Roger, about to light his cigar, became motionless. If he had not been abruptly reminded—he had no idea how—of his Hallowe'en fiasco with Helene, or even if Macher had not gone on interestedly looking at him, he would probably not have said:

'If I may just revert to what we were saying a moment ago, Mr. Macher, I'd like to suggest that one reason why you were dissatisfied with what I was saying to Father Colgate might be that through no fault of your own you're simply not qualified to appreciate the subtleties of a discussion between Christians.'

His tone rather than his words brought a momentary silence. Then Hirsch said: 'I guess I'll go eat' and went. The youth possibly called Page had time to say: 'Now look, sir, around here we don't make hostile references to—' before the one probably called Castlemaine broke in and said: 'Excuse me, Mr. Micheldene, but is it permissible to ask you a personal question?'

'By all means.'

'Thank you, sir. In that case I should very much like

to know whether, as it appears, you propose to smoke that cigar while the band is still around it.'

'The band?'

'The circle of coloured paper, sir, near the smoking end.'

'Oh, the ring. How dense of me. Yes, naturally I shall leave it there while I smoke,' Roger said, starting to. 'Why do you ask?'

'I know very little about these things, sir, having been raised in Philadelphia, but around there I've noticed that people who are about to smoke a cigar invariably remove the . . . the ring before lighting it. Would you say it was . . . wrong of them to do this?'

'Oh no, not wrong, no no, that's taking the thing far too seriously.' Roger spoke with animation. Having scored his point against Macher he was not unwilling to pass to other spheres, especially since he was half aware that some judges might consider that point to have been scored at some sacrifice. Never call a Jew a Jew unless you can be sure of making him lose his temper by doing so—a sound rule which the memory of Helene had flustered him into breaking. For so far from having become angry, Macher was now looking at him with something oddly resembling friendliness.

Castlemaine seemed to be pondering. 'Then perhaps . . . socially inept?'

'Hardly that either. Removing the ring before lighting is just a fairly harmless modern affectation, as well as involving the risk of damaging the binder—the outside leaf, that is.'

'I appreciate that point.'

'By the time you've smoked a cigar down as far as the ring you'll have had the best out of it anyway. It's by way of being a little theory of mine that the position of the ring is a reminder to the smoker that he's reached the stage of, let's say, diminishing returns. But I can't seem to find any support in cigar literature.'

'How curious.'

'Now I'm afraid that right here I must interrupt this interesting discussion and carry off our good friend Mr. Micheldene in the direction of his speaking engagement for this evening.' This was delivered more slowly than any other possessor of approximately normal speech organs would consider. But then Maynard Parrish always talked like that. Dressed in a bottle-green suit that shone—by design, it was plain, not through excessive wear—he had long finished arriving and nodding thoroughly to each under-graduate in turn by the time his voice finally died away.

It seemed as good a time as any. Roger offered a token farewell to Macher's group, but was surprised to find some or all of it accompanying him and Parrish towards the entrance. On the way an opening door afforded a glimpse of a detachment of the U.S. Cavalry charging across a television screen in full colour and half a dozen recumbent shapes grouped round. There was a lot of thick carpeting about in the hall, heavy leather upholstery and more dark panelling. This and the chromium-and-strip-lighting thing were about the only two styles they knew.

Roger picked up his briefcase from the unnecessarily elaborate cloakroom, felt momentary but active hatred for a group of men in knickerbockers and such whose photograph hung near the front door, and allowed himself to be led across the road to a similar building. Headlights and neon lit his path. Indoors again he dealt with a stair or so and some corridor, overcorrecting rather at the bends. Weak liquor was not an American shortcoming. Then he was in an ante-room affair with about twenty people. He was assured that one of them was the editor of the town newspaper and another the editor of the campus newspaper. That was to be expected, but what did Father Colgate think he was doing here? And who were all these women?

CHAPTER IX

ROGER WAS STILL pondering on the Colgate and women problems when he opened his briefcase to take out the material of his lecture. This he had compiled with some labour, promising himself that Helene (who had definitely undertaken to attend) should get her money's worth of him in his role as man of affairs, understander of the way the world worked, unearther of significant facts and such. To this end he had equipped himself not only with detailed notes but with published material from which he proposed to read extracts. The whole thing formed a substantial sheaf of typescript and print, from which the single slim pamphlet-like affair which was all his briefcase now proved to contain could immediately be distinguished.

He found himself looking hard at what he took to be a child's comic. On its cover was the garishly coloured carica-ture of a small boy with a more compulsively kickable face than any even Roger could have visualised unaided. The back of his neck went cold and his face hot. 'Look at this,' he managed to say to Parrish, who had time to gaze at it with senatorial benevolence and say : 'Yes, a most—' before Roger charged on with : 'Can't you understand? Some-body's stolen my lecture notes and stuck this piece of . . . piece of . . .'

He raved more or less inarticulately for a time while the others milled about him, inquiring, sympathising, exclaim-ing, soothing. But a part of his mind was clear. The child in the drawing had directed his thoughts to another whose odiousness was inward, or at any rate not primarily facial.

Before leaving the Bangs' house a couple of hours earlier he had put his briefcase on a table near the front door and Arthur had asked what was in it and Roger had told him it was his lecture. Then, he remembered in detail, he had gone back to his room to change his tie. The regimental one he had originally selected was on reflection too ordinary-looking at a distance and he had spent some time tying a green Paisley bow—quite long enough for that inventive miniature fiend to make the switch. But this realisation, convincing as it was, failed to draw Roger's anger away from those immediately round him. It was his habit in such situations to blaze away at any human target that might move across his sights, as many a London waiter, hotel servant and telephone operator could have testified. Shaking his fist for silence, he said :

'I'd like somebody to go as soon as possible, please, and inform the audience that I shan't be appearing before them.'

'But surely—'

'It isn't fair to keep people hanging about.'

'But there must be upward of a hundred and fifty—'

'I don't care if there's a hundred thousand, they'll simply have to do without me, I'm afraid.'

'But you can't just flatly refuse to—'

'Can't I? By what incapacity can I not? It isn't my fault, is it? Be so good as to remember that. It isn't my fault.'

'Now, Roger, my old friend,' Maynard Parrish said in the voice that had reduced so many stormy departmental meetings to universal undifferentiated apathy, 'let's just see if we can't devise some means of salvaging something out of this admittedly most difficult and unfortunate situation. For my own part I undertake—'

'There's nothing to be done. I'm not talking and that's that.'

'Roger, please, one moment. You—and I say this, believe me, in no spirit of flattery—you are one of the most articulate and verbally resourceful men it has ever been my good fortune to hold converse with. Surely it cannot be beyond the powers of one such as you to improvise a—'

'If you think I'm going out there to give those people a fifty-minute impromptu chat you're doomed to disappointment. They might not be able to tell the difference between that and a serious lecture but I can. I won't do it.'

'If I were to announce a half-hour delay, during which period you could set your thoughts in—'

'No.'

Roger said this so ardently that there was a sudden silence in the room and even, possibly, in the auditorium that lay on the far side of a pair of manorial swing doors. Parrish, Macher and a couple of his friends, the two editors, half a dozen women in their fifties who looked as if they could have slogged it out blow for blow with Roger over any number of rounds he cared to name, Father Colgate, all watched him as he made to hurl the comic book to the floor, then changed his mind and stuffed it into his briefcase.

'I hope you'll dine with me, Roger?' Parrish said.

'Don't count on it. I'll telephone you. And now, if you'll all excuse me, I really must be going.'

In the entrance hall Roger became aware that somebody had hurried after him from the ante-room. It was Father Colgate, who said urgently to him : 'I must say something urgently to you.'

'I doubt whether it would strike me as urgent, Father, but whatever it is it'll have to—'

'In my calling one very quickly develops what might almost be called an instinct whereby he comes to detect infallibly the signs of a soul at variance with God. You, my son, are very gravely disturbed. You are in acute spiritual

pain—the infallible sign of a soul at variance with God. I
detected this from your very violent and distraught words
to me back in the fraternity house and I obtained the
clearest possible confirmation from the way you behaved a
moment ago. A man doesn't act like a child unless his soul
is hurting him. Your soul is hurting you, Mr. Micheldene.
Won't you allow me to hear your confession, my son?
Soon. The sooner the better.'

What had kept Roger quiet through this was a series of
inner debates about how hard, where and how soon he
ought to strike the speaker. But now the pause tempted
him into speech. 'I'm not your son, you dog-collared
buffoon,' he said confidently, 'and I wouldn't confess to you
if I had a rope round my neck. Now unless you want to
be martyred in the next five seconds you get out of my
way.'

'Resistance to the will of God is the surest—'

'It's the will of God that I have a large strong drink
immediately and nobody had better resist that. Good-
evening to you. Oh, and pray for me, won't you, Father?
It'll do you good.'

Roger had three large strong drinks sitting up at the
counter in a place along the street. 'You're English, aren't
you?' the barman asked.

'Yes.'

'I was in England during the war. You know South-
ampton?'

'No.'

'So I talk too much already. Go ahead, commune with
yourself.'

Roger's self-communion brought him the unhelpful
thought that by delivering an impromptu talk, not for him
a very difficult task, he might have impressed Helene more
than by lecturing as planned—assuming, he added to himself gloomily, that he was capable of impressing her at all

by that sort of thing, or any sort of thing. Then he medi-
tated upon Arthur. The briefcase coup had called for a
combination of inventiveness, malignity and daring surprising in one so young. Or was it surprising? An arch-
criminal on the scale Arthur was destined to attain must
surely reveal himself early. Galileo, Columbus, Clement
Attlee, Caxton had all had childhoods. It suddenly occurred
to him to be astonished at the magnitude of his love for
Helene. If she left Ernst and came to him she would presumably bring Arthur with her, and here he was still trying
to persuade her. But this, for some reason, turned out to
be another unwelcome line of thought.

He finished his drink with a silent toast to Herod, then
telephoned for a taxi. The promptitude with which he was
connected and promised service and given it nettled him
vaguely, but he could think of no more acceptable alternative. 'Good-night, Claud,' the barman said.

Back at the Bangs' he found Helene sitting reading a
women's magazine by a small log fire, a cup of coffee at
her elbow. She was wearing sandals with gilt straps, striped
slacks, and a lemon-coloured cardigan of coarse wool that
offered hints about her figure, as opposed to the forthright
statements of fact set out by her usual sweaters and blouses.
Her cheeks were pink, her expression as sleepily cheerful as
ever. She turned a page and said: 'Hallo, you're back
early. How did it go?'

'How did it go? You weren't there?'

'No, I'm terribly sorry, I did try, but our regular baby-
sitter had a paper to finish in the library and I couldn't
get hold of anybody else that late. I did try. How'd it go,
anyhow?'

'Go? It didn't go. There was no lecture.'

Ernst, a disassembled mechanical toy in his hand, came
through the doorway from the kitchen in time to hear this.
He seemed surprised. Helene put her magazine down and

looked for a cigarette. 'Why not? Are you sick or something? What happened?'

'No, I'm perfectly all right,' Roger said. In fact he felt dashed by Helene's evident unconcern to attend his talk (what would have prevented Ernst from baby-sitting, for instance?), but he was not really surprised by it. And he was confident of being able to get the maximum anti-Arthur value out of his impending revelations without loss of composure. Rage was always fun, true, but it had been known to lower efficiency and, in particular, parents tended on the whole to resent its being directed against their children by outsiders.

While Ernst and Helene first exchanged a glance and then watched him, he proceeded with due pomp to the cobbler's bench, set his briefcase down there and opened it. Slowly he drew from it the comic book, which he held up so that his audience could see it clearly, then cleared his throat as if really about to lecture. 'This,' he said—'this was what I found when I went to take out my notes and so forth before I went on to the platform this evening. The notes had disappeared—though I'm pretty sure I know roughly where they are. We'll go into that in a minute. At any rate, it thereupon became obviously impossible for me to appear, I said as much to that old nitwit Parrish, went and had a couple of drinks in some bar or other and made my way back here. I told Parrish I might dine with him later as arranged but I don't really feel like it.'

Helene said diffidently: 'But couldn't you have just gone on and said something off the cuff? It was to be about publishing, wasn't it? Well, surely you must have a lot of that right at your fingertips—quite enough for a—'

'No, Helene,' Ernst said, 'Roger is completely right here. One's method of preparation in each case is entirely different. If one has organised one's material into a formal script of some kind, one has an attitude to it which—'

'But all those people who'd come along, they were expecting—'

'—possibility of talking informally, which of course with due warning—'

'—not all that critical, they'd have been quite content with—'

'—actually militates against any kind of improvised—'

'—sending them home without even—'

'—something one can't simply—'

'—tough on everybody.'

'—like television.'

Roger decided it was time he resumed control. 'Be that as it may,' he said, 'what interests me most at the moment is who was responsible for this little . . . prank.'

'Any theories, Mr. District Attorney?' Helene asked.

'Yes, I have. I'm going to be quite blunt about this.' Roger's voice was gentle. He even smiled. 'I connect children's comics with children. As far as I know only one child had the chance to get at my briefcase after I put my script into it. Arthur.'

'But he wouldn't do a thing like this,' Helene said with animation, and Ernst shook his head hard.

'He asked me what was in here, and I said my lecture, and I left it unattended for a few minutes, and there you are.'

'But why would he—?' Helene began.

Ernst took over: 'Now Roger, please consider this point. You told Arthur your briefcase contained your lecture, correct? Just reflect for a moment what the concept *lecture* means to a young child. If indeed he has that concept at all. A lecture to him is something that happens, something that his parents and people go to. Like a concert, let's say. As adults we're used to the abstract shift whereby a lecture as well as being an activity becomes an object, a number of pieces of paper that can be carried about or even printed and bound. This kind of semantic relocation is such a familiar feature of our language that its boldness no longer—'

'Let me have a look at that thing,' Helene said to Roger. 'But this is *Crazy* magazine, not a comic book. Kids don't read this—not kids of Arthur's age. It's way beyond them. Far too sophisticated.'

'Arthur's remarkably intelligent,' Roger said. 'We all agree on that.'

'Not this intelligent. This stuff is satire.'

'Oh, satire.' Roger spoke as if of mentholated snuff or an African politician. 'I thought they got that given away free with their teething rings these days. Anyway, there are pictures and monsters and things in this thing, aren't there? Quite enough to interest a kid like—'

'Well, you wouldn't know about that, would you, Roger?'

'May I see?' Ernst asked. He began a careful study.

'There's one very simple way of settling all this,' Roger said, still gently. 'I'm still perfectly certain in my own mind that Arthur's responsible, but I can see you and Ernst don't agree. Let's see what Arthur has to say about it, shall we?'

'Oh, sure, I'll mention it to him in the morning, but I can't see—'

'I don't mean in the morning. I mean now.'

Helene's elongated light-grey eyes had been looking at him with mild concern and a sort of neutral wonder. Now her gaze sharpened and she opened and shut her mouth. 'Roger, he's asleep. It's late.'

'Nonsense, it's only . . . five-and-twenty to nine. If I'm wrong or we get nowhere then no very great harm will have been done. Whereas if I'm right, and I don't think there's any *if* about it, he'll be taught a very valuable lesson. It'll be impressed on his mind.'

She put her hand on his arm. 'Now listen, I know

you're upset about this but you must see reason. I am not about to go and wake up that child and drag him on out here and have him accused of something he won't even be able to understand. You won't shift me on this one.'

Roger shook off her hand. He said nothing, but his expression made her turn violently away. Then Ernst, forgotten by both of them for the last minute, broke into a shout of laughter which he renewed at intervals.

'Oh, just look at this,' he said as best he could. 'How excellent. Oh, this is really rich. The forensic laboratory failed to examine the evidence closely enough. Child suspect cleared. There, at the bottom.'

On the back page of the magazine, in smudged but legible blue lettering, were the words: *Property of Rho Epsilon Chi Fraternity: not to be removed from reading room.*

Roger's facial muscles went out of control for a moment while Ernst continued laughing and Helene, after some hesitation, joined in. The lack of malice in their laughter made things worse. Soon abandoning the search for an utterance or (short of throwing himself through the picture window) an action large enough to express his feelings, Roger set about laughing too. The fluctuating bray which was all he could come up with at first evidently passed muster. Ernst put his arm round Helene and went on laughing and saying:

'So the childish innocent was spared in the nick of time. Escaped being put to the sword. You were certainly breathing fire and slaughter when you came in, Roger. I honestly believe if we hadn't been here Arthur would have paid the supreme penalty already. Oh, what a real yell.'

'The laugh's certainly on me,' Roger said, keeping his mouth expanded and producing an aspirated grunt every half-second or so.

Ernst now visibly pulled himself together, rolling his

arms and shoulders and neck about. 'But that's enough of that. Joke over. This is a serious matter. Either you have an enemy or there's a rather unbalanced practical joker around. Perhaps both. We must decide what's to be done. Let's all have a drink and talk about it.'

When Ernst had gone to the kitchen Roger said: 'It was just that I couldn't see how anybody else could have done it.'

'Sure, I know.'

'I didn't mean I thought he was terribly wicked or any-thing like that.'

'Of course not.'

'Kids get up to all sorts of games, don't they?'

'Yeah.'

For the next minute Roger worked hard at convincing himself that now was not the time for a quick query about his chances of getting into bed with Helene over the week-end. Conversation stopped. Helene went and looked for her cigarettes. As soon as Ernst came back with the drinks, his face showing that he had done some hard thinking in the meantime, Roger realised he would not be able to stand three hours of careful speculation about the identity of the magazine-criminal.

What he got instead, after a speedy telephone call and another taxi, was five hours of Maynard Parrish and his guests. They had waited dinner for him, but all eleven other members of the company had time to drink a final cocktail and say something different about his non-lecture. Their puzzlement seemed inexhaustible in its profusion and variety. He sat between a female professor of international law and the French-speaking wife of a Turkish art his-torian. Then in the drawing-room the men got together and went carefully through the Administration's farming policy, winding up with a brief fiscal survey.

Roger was feeling more tired than drunk as he stood in

the Bangs' drive and the man who had driven him there rolled his window down and said: 'Your basic objection to Jack Kennedy appears to be that he's an American. Don't think I don't sympathise, but unfortunately we have this law here that says the President of the United States has to be a citizen of the Republic. Unreasonable, I grant you, but there it is. *Dura lex sed lex*, old man, which is Iroquois for Why don't you go back to your island and stay there. Good-night.'

The sound of the car had perhaps awakened the Bangs, whose bedroom was next to Roger's. At any rate, shiftings and murmurings could be heard. Not bothering to get on his knees, Roger made a few silent remarks to Jehovah on the events of the evening as he undressed and got into bed. He was nearly asleep when the sounds on the other side of the wooden wall took shape. They went on for some time. Putting his fingers in his ears helped surprisingly little. He found he could just about stand it while Helene's voice came from closed lips. Certainly it was a good deal harder to bear whenever he heard her mouth open. He tried all he could, but in vain, to remember whether it had ever been like that when he was with her.

Lying on his stomach, he put one pillow each side of his head and pressed violently inward with his fists. 'Not now,' he said. 'As much as they like when I'm not here, but not now. Please.'

CHAPTER X

The instant Roger woke up the next morning he remembered in exact detail what he had heard through his bedroom wall. The thought of it lay in his mind without moving, without generating other thoughts, simply *there*. The surrounding silence told him it was still early but, with his pocket watch unreachably far away in his jacket across the room, he had no way of knowing how early. What he could see through the window without raising his head told him nothing. The wire mesh of the screen gave the view a mealy, pointilliste quality, like a representation of what a dog sees.

He tried to doze. Each time he began to succeed he had the illusion that thin metal sheets were being gently pounded with some padded object nearby. The sound died away in a whisper as soon as he directed his attention to it. After a few goes of this he fell quite asleep again and dreamed vividly. Now and then the dreams took a turn which pushed him back into consciousness with no memory in his head, only incredulity that such a thing could ever have taken place in a human brain. This incredulity grew sharper at every awakening until at last he half sat up with a jerk, vainly trying to recall why.

He got out of bed and padded to the window. Viewed from here the scene looked different. It reflected a fair amount of sunlight but in a dull, uniform way, as if everything—neighbours' houses, lawns scattered with fallen leaves, gravel roadway, thin evergreen copse—had been sprayed with a thin film of gelatin. There was nobody about.

A sensation stirred deep within his nose, half tickle, half prickle. He rubbed it cautiously, then rotated his facial muscles, wincing. A gradual probe with the little finger left no room for doubt. He was afflicted with double snuff-taker's nostril, a malady that lined the nasal mucous membrane with hard, sharp, embedded particles of snot. The effect was of a pair of wasp-sized hedgehogs having crawled up his nose and decided to stay. They would hang about there, he knew from experience, for the next week at least. His tolerance must be diminishing—a sign, perhaps, of advancing age—because he had not taken all that much last night. Finding himself one down at Parrish's place after a discussion of Britain's independent nuclear deterrent he had fought back by producing all his boxes in quick succession and, interest aroused or at any rate simulated, delivering his standard snuff lecture : historical sketch, method of manufacture, variety of blends, anecdote about accidental discovery of High Dry Toast process, etc. He had quelled a threatened interruption from a social scientist with information about oral snuff-taking on the Ohio riverboats by pressing on him a hefty pinch of Seville—'a good sharp sniff is what you need to get the best out of it' —and throughout the man's ensuing forty-minute sneezing fit had felt bound to demonstrate his own immunity by getting rid of about a saltspoonful twice a minute. Strong stuff, Seville. He dislodged some of the bulkier fragments now with his nail and pushed up each nostril a fat gout of the skinfood he sometimes remembered to smear round his eyes last thing at night.

His watch said eight o'clock. He dressed with torpid movements, becoming animated only when confronted by the clean shirt, a broad-striped lilac and white affair, he proposed to put on. This had been laundered with suspicious promptitude by a very small shop round the corner from his borrowed apartment, and its packaging stoutly

resisted entry. Cardboard, several sorts of plastic, pins—he
ripped and tugged and flung for a good minute, marvelling
at the detachment whereby he was able to imagine the
shouts and howls Joe Derlanger would produce in this
situation. Roger found himself almost looking forward to
seeing Joe at the monstrous party (oh, why did they have
to keep having them? Why was going to parties the only
thing any of them ever did?) that Ernst had fixed up for tonight. Joe had something of the child in him, a grave
demerit, but he was a man of fair education, or what passed
for that over here, and the speed with which he identified
and combated any force retrograde to his own will was a
mark of distinction. It was an experience to hear him re-
sisting Grace's proposed mealtimes and menus, never producing the same objection twice in an evening : too much
too late at night, none of this fancy French stuff, not ham-
burgers again, perhaps after another couple of drinks, only
with genuine veal-marrow stock. Going hungry for an hour
or two during this was a penalty even Roger was prepared
to pay.

He put on his Royal Windrush Yacht Club blazer and
left the house, tiptoeing past Arthur's bedroom, from which
came yelps of an unidentified emotion and the sound of
miniature wheeled vehicles. The sky was pale blue and the
air already mild : this year's Indian summer, so they all kept
assuring him, was going to break records. Perhaps everybody would not, as he half hoped they would, freeze to
death after all on this barge that was to provide the venue
for this evening's romp. Barge? With a concept like that,
of course, they might jump in either of their two favourite
opposite directions. Would the *barge* turn out to be some
funnelless yacht boasting a uniformed crew and two or
three bars hung with abstract expressionist paintings?
Rather more likely he would find middle-aged men in jeans
and leather jackets doling out martinis from the middle of

a waterlogged raft, an authentic Mississippi relic trans-
ported in sections across a thousand miles of land for the
occasion. Could they never do things except by two-and-a-
halves?

Before these riddles could be answered there was the rest
of the day to be got through. Breakfast *à quatre*, featuring
Arthur Bang, monologuist and domestic acrobat, would be
the first ordeal. As soon as possible thereafter Roger planned
to retreat to his bedroom and stay there until as soon as
possible before lunch. He had work to do, he had said, and
had noticed on his return last night that someone had
carried in there for the purpose a small desk battered into
seeming antiquity. He had indeed a few proof copies to look
through, but the main business of his morning was going
to be the composition of a long letter to his current wife,
Pamela, saying among other things that he saw no objection to taking her out to dinner and talking matters over
with her when he returned to England.

There was a good deal to be said against Pamela, as nobody knew better than he. He remembered her mother
warning him, that day at Ascot, how highly strung the
girl was, how difficult to deal with. She was a great one
for imaginary slights, bursting into tears if he should as
much as venture to correct her grammar or point out that
her reading an occasional manuscript for him when he was
too busy was no excuse for skimping the *sauce vinaigrette*
when they gave one of their dinner parties. She had even
complained—once—that he was selfish in bed. On the other
hand, she was decorative, knew a lot of people and could
carry on a serious discussion in the intervals of mistaking
differences of opinion for him being beastly to her. The real
trouble was that times like the present, when, for some
reason he could not pin down, he rather fancied the idea
of a reconciliation, tended to coincide with the times when,
just as unaccountably, he rather fancied the idea of getting

on terms with the Church again. And the Church, when consulted, had always said that according to it he was still married to his first wife, Marigold. And knowing the Church was wrong, emotionally wrong, wrong by any standard but the most literal and obscurantist, somehow did not help.

Well, anyway, reading and writing would keep him going until well after the start of the midday drinks session, at which he was going to be able, should he feel like it, to further his acquaintance with the Fraschini-Sullivan-Selby-Green group. Later there would be a serve-yourself meal, after which they would all try to get him to go with them to the afternoon's football game, Budweiser vs. Ballantine —not such an important event, they would explain, as next week's Budweiser-Rheingold encounter, but none the less likely to be pretty damn interesting and surely he would not want to pass up the chance of seeing some real college football. (He had had all this several times over *chez* Rho Epsilon Chi the previous evening.) The next stage would be a sample, as protracted as he dared, of his favourite mock-indecision act, full of references to work, expected telephone calls and such. Finally he would regretfully decline and the football party, including Ernst, would move off. And then . . .

With the sun faintly warm on the back of his neck he strolled through long grass towards the spot where he had seen the deer earlier that week. This brought him to a small wooden hut with a red and green pennant saying *BUDWEISER* nailed above its door. He peered inside and saw evidence of childish occupancy: wet and tattered comic books, food fragments, a plastic belt and holster, a clockwork robot fifteen inches high. This last he picked up, noting that it seemed in good repair, and carried to an open space. From here, first glancing carefully up at the house, he hurled it with all his strength into a well-overgrown patch of woodland at the corner of the property. It disappeared with a rustle and a faint snapping of stems. That will teach little men to cheat their elders at tomfool word games, he thought to himself. Then he turned away and walked up towards the road.

As he went he kept his eyes open for flowers, which were one item in the external world he could honestly say he liked. But, as might have been expected, there were none about. People here only valued them as sex-cum-affluence tokens and sent girls orchids they had never seen and would barely recognise as such if they did. Nobody was interested in having flowers just growing round the place: who would bother to plant and tend a rose-bed when he could have a Cadillac delivered in an hour? Roger thought bitterly of the rose-garden behind Marrano, the house near Sevenoaks he and Pamela had lived in for five years—when she left him it had seemed (and, without her money, had in fact been) uneconomic to keep it up and he had had to sell it to a Jew who trafficked in ski-wear for women. What would a fellow like that see in the huge yellow Mermaids and heavy-scented Etoiles d'Hollande that would be out at this very moment, let alone the more distinguished summer shrubs, the Rosamundae, the white moss roses of which Bill Sussex had once remarked that he wished he had anything half so good of its kind in his own gardens? Roger visualised himself at Marrano now, in his hand the secateurs Wilkinsons had made for him, planning his buttonholes for next week or explaining the historical interest of certain old-fashioned varieties to a likely young woman.

In his preoccupation he nearly tripped over some wretched creeper that, for want of a fence or anything to climb up, was sprawling about on the ground. Its leaves looked sticky and were a purplish dark green in colour, like an artichoke's that is starting to go off. Roger glared at it. So this was the best they could do. It just showed how . . .

A voice called: 'Hi.' Roger looked up and saw a man, perhaps the man called Selby, smiling and waving at him from the next-door garden. He wore a shirt with a huge grey and yellow check pattern. Roger nodded and moved up towards the Bangs' kitchen door before Selby could rush at him and thrust into his hands a typewritten slip with the Latin name of the creeper on it and a map showing its distribution in North America.

In the kitchen Helene was preparing breakfast, starting, specifically, to fry bacon that she was soon to drain on a paper towel and render so brittle that the mere act of serving would disintegrate it. But as yet Roger knew, and would have cared, nothing about this. Helene smiled cheerfully at him through the window and he looked back at her, aware that he had not yet thought of her that morning in any direct way at all, let alone as someone who might be going to bed with him that afternoon. Even while he voiced this idea to himself—taking in as he did so Helene's pale-blue-and-white-striped housecoat and the total disarray of her hair, which consequently ranged in appearance from fur to cloudy wire—he felt its reality slipping away from him. It was like abandoning a theory for lack of evidence. And surely he had never seriously imagined that he could induce her to... but he managed to block off that one (the long-term one) before it could cross his mental threshold.

So unwilling had he suddenly become to encounter Helene that he considered hanging about outside for a few more minutes in the hope that the rest of the household would arrive to dilute her. This was for him an unusual reaction, especially considering who was the potential diluter-in-chief. He abandoned the idea on seeing and hearing that Selby had moved round to the front of his house and was now exchanging humorous democratic shouts with the mail-man and an elderly Negro who was sweeping dead leaves off the driveway of the house opposite.

He went inside and, at the promptings of some myster-
ious instinct, greeted Helene cordially. Then he drank
orange-juice at a temperature and in a quantity that would
have given him, had he been Roger Micheldene's stomach,
just cause to hit Roger Micheldene hard in the mouth.
After that he put down half a dozen hot pancakes with
maple syrup as well as the fragmented bacon, several ounces
of Iowa-Idaho quince preserve on rye bread, and four
cups of coffee. The total effect made him feel jaunty enough
to light one of his crooked black Honduras cheroots and
pat Arthur gently on the head before going back to his
room and skimming through a piece of grandiose sublit-
eracy about inarticulate wisdom in Kentucky.

The next four or five hours passed as he had expected. At
the end of them he said to Helene : 'Are we going to be
able to go to bed this afternoon?'

'Honey, I'm afraid it'd be terribly difficult.'

'Yes, I thought it might be.'

'You see, as a rule I'd be able to fix it with Sue Green to
have Arthur, but Russ and Linda went to New York to
their grandparents' this weekend and Clay took Sue to the
game and afterward they're having cocktails with the
Oxenreiders—he's the coach—and Jimmy Fraschini seems
to have dropped over, and ordinarily I could have told
them to go play around the Fraschinis' place, but I don't
think I could really do that this afternoon because Arthur's
having tea there tomorrow.'

'Yes, I see. Bit of a bore that Arthur isn't going out to
tea today instead of tomorrow.'

'I know it, but . . . it didn't work out that way.'

'No.'

'So I guess it looks as if . . .'

'Yes. Well, I think in that case I'll go and seek my own
chaste couch for an hour or two, if you'll excuse me. I
didn't sleep too well last night.'

For the twentieth time in the last half-hour Roger heard
the slam of the screen door and the thunder of tiny feet as
Arthur and his confederate entered the house to fetch some
article of play or else simply entered. Roger had noticed—
nobody in Arthur's general neighbourhood could help noticing—that the child had no special interest in being indoors,
any more than in being outdoors. What interested him
very much was coming indoors, especially straight into a
room of conversing adults. Sometimes, as now, he would
employ a variant whereby a random commotion about the
house preluded his abrupt arrival by an inner door. But to
be already talking fast and loud when he crossed the threshold, in entreaty, protest, self-praise or simple narrative, was
an unchanging feature.

Helene had been looking curiously at Roger for about a
second and a half when Arthur made his entry saying:
'Mommy, someone stole Robert, I left him guarding the
station in the wood and now he isn't there any more, so
someone must have—'

'Will you be quiet, Arthur? Mr. Micheldene and I are
talking.'

'Mommy, I just told you someone stole Robert, you've
got to help me look—'

'Got to nothing. Now out. Take off, child. You and your
buddy both.' Helene got up and began pushing her son
backwards towards the doorway. 'Just disappear and hurry
up about it.'

'Mommy . . .' Arthur's gaze settled on Roger and filled
with silent and hopeless accusation.

'Get vaporised before I kill you,' Helene said, shoving
harder and more effectively. She slammed the door. Then
she turned slowly and Roger, in the midst of approving the
small but notable advance just made in family relations,
saw curiosity return to her face. Looking elegant, or as
nearly elegant as she ever got, in a dark-blue rough-silk

dress, she walked over to where he was sitting and stood quite close. After a moment she said: 'Why aren't you angry with me?'

'Angry with you? Because the arrangements haven't worked out? Why should that make me angry with you? You did your best, didn't you?'

'But that sort of thing doesn't usually make any difference to . . .' She paused, frowning. 'I mean, ordinarily you just—'

'I agree this sort of thing does make me frightfully angry as a rule, yes, but somehow not today.'

'What's so special about today?'

'Well, I rather fancy the answer to that must be that in my heart of hearts, as it were, I never reallly quite got to the point of believing it was going to happen at all. So when I found out the whole thing had fallen through I wasn't really surprised. Only being told what I knew already.'

While he was saying this Helene had winced sharply and started to gnaw the inside of her lips. Blinking fast, she stared out of the picture-window. 'There's the zoo,' she said, indistinctly because she had a fingernail between her teeth.

'The zoo?'

'Well it's hardly a zoo at all really. There's a giraffe and some kind of ape, but the rest is all muskrats and foxes and coyotes and things. The main attraction's the bear hunt.'

'The bear hunt?'

'Well, naturally it isn't a regular bear hunt. There's no bear. At least they do have this mangy old grizzly chained up to a tree but they don't hunt it. All they do, they ride their ponies through the wood to where the bear is and then they kind of ride around it for a bit. Then they can have a hamburger, I guess. It'll give us a clear hour or so anyway. If I know young Martha Selby she'll do the whole job for five dollars inclusive.'

CHAPTER XI

'*CONTICUERE OMNES,*' ROGER was saying urgently to himself half an hour later, '*intentique ora tenebant. Inde toro pater Aeneas sic fatus ab alto: "Infandum, regina, iubes renovare dolorem; sed ...*" No, it's ... Hell: *colle sub aprico celeberrimus ilice lucus ...* Trouble with the damned stuff it's all chopped up into lengths so you have to know the beginning of every line and never get a clue out of what's gone before. Oh God—*hic haec hoc hic-haec-hoc* yes yes yes now *hunc hanc hoc* three *huiuses* three *huics hoc hac hoc* right *his hae ha ... Ha? Ha ha ha horum his his?* That can't be right, can it? No, of course, it's *haec*, you idiot. Get on with it—*hi hae haec* then straight on to the Greek irregulars *esthio* and good old *blosko-moloumai* yes now back to *hi hae haec hos has hos* three *horums ...*'

What Roger was saying to himself might have struck a casual observer, if one could have been contrived, as greatly at variance with what he was doing. In fact, however, the two were intimately linked. If he wanted to go on doing what he was doing for more than another ten seconds at the outside it was essential that he should go on saying things to himself—any old things as long as the supply of them could be kept up. Nothing else at hand suggested itself as a means of self-distraction. Very early in his career (he had only been troubled in this way a couple of times since then) he had found himself reading the better part of a chapter of Evelyn Waugh's book on Rossetti in this situation, rather to the puzzlement and, after a time, to the irritation of his companion, an Irish waitress from the considerably worse of the two local hotels. The episode had done nothing to alleviate his generally harsh view of Pre-Raphaelite theory and practice, notably its religiose aspects.

His present difficulty with Helene was partly inherent in her, but could be traced more immediately to the prolonged bout of anticipation he had endured before she had rounded up the three children involved, dumped them at the zoo place and driven back to the house. Then there had been the moment when her usual policy of bodily self-effacement seemed to slip her mind and he was paid back twice over for everything he had missed the day by the swimming-pool. He found it hard to drive that out of his head, or to want to. Not the memory of seeing Arthur being got into the car, with a liberal helping hand from behind that brought him down on hands and knees, not even self-admiration at having managed Helene with such imagination and resource was any use to him. He kept having to fall back on this Latin and Greek and stuff.

All was very nearly lost when he found that *esthio* and *blosko*, though all right as far as they went, pointed nowhere much. He struggled halfway through the paradigm of *horao* with his mind becoming progressively blanker. 'Oh Jesus,' his internal monologue continued, 'whan that Aprill with his shoures sote the droght of March hath perced to the rote, and bathed every vein in swich licour, of which vertu engendred is the flour, then . . . then *whoops*—the weeping Pleiads wester and the moon is under seas; from bourne to bourne of midnight far sighs the rainy breeze. It sighs from a lost country to a land I have not known; the weeping Pleiads wester and . . . the moon is under seas, that's more like it, from bourne to bourne . . .'

After the weeping Pleiads had made half a dozen circuits he found things beginning to get easier. His mind stopped behaving like a motor with a slipping clutch and gradually withdrew into itself. He saw nothing; there were

sounds, but he heard them less and less. He lost all interest in where he was and who he was with, in any part or
aspect of the future. For perhaps a minute, though he himself could not have known how long, he came as close as
he had ever done to being unaware of who he was. Then
the minute ended and he began taking notice of things
again, including who he was with. The memory of how he
had felt combined with elation at having done what he
had been at such pains to do and induced him to give up
more of his time to the final blandishments than he normally cared to. One of the really good ones, he thought.

Helene propped her head on her elbow and stared at
him. She was flushed and tousled now all right. 'It was nice
for you, wasn't it?' she said with little inquiry.

'Of course, my dear, perfectly splendid, I assure you.
Why, wasn't it nice for you?'

'Oh yes.'

'Good.'

'You get what you want quite a lot of the time, don't
you?'

'I most certainly do not. Quite the contrary, in fact.
Whatever gave you that idea? If I got a bit more of what
I wanted I might be rather easier to handle.'

'Oh, so you know you're not easy to handle?'

'Of course. Demonstrably I'm not.'

'Why do you want to do this so much?'

'What, this? Is that a mystery? You're absolutely simply
and unequivocally the most attractive woman I've ever
laid eyes on, let alone managed to get my—'

'That's good to hear, honey, but I didn't mean with me
personally, I meant with everybody. That's who you really
want, isn't it? everybody?'

'Fortunately, perhaps, there are certain immutable limita-
tions in the structure of things which render the consum-
mation of any such ambition beyond one's grasp.'

'Sure, sure, old thing, but it is everybody you want, isn't it?'

'God, I don't know. It's possible, I suppose. But then I've never managed to have anybody I really wanted for long enough, you see. If I did I might turn out to be much better about wanting everybody. I don't know.'

'What about your wives? Didn't you really want them? Or did you not have them for long enough?'

'Christ, it certainly wasn't that. A total of twelve years, thanks most awfully. No, I imagine I must not really have wanted them. I certainly thought I did when I started off, got to admit that. That's one of the snags.'

'What is?' She had the sheet wrapped half round her, tucked neatly under her armpits. Her tanned skin looked nice against it, but Roger could think of nicer alternative arrangements without having to rack his brains.

'Well,' he said, 'it's such a long time between getting hold of somebody and finding out if you really wanted them in the first place. Like love at first sight. You can only tell if that's happened by what happens afterwards.'

'Oh, maybe, but we're getting away from the subject. What is it about women that makes you want them? And please, no biology lesson.'

'Well, I think it's all most frightfully obscure really.' Roger did not go on to try to describe how he had felt for that minute or so just now, because it failed to cross his mind. He was no better than the next man at remembering, or at knowing, why he did things. He had lied to Helene. Whether or not his motives about women were obscure he did not think they were. A man's sexual aim, he had often said to himself, is to convert a creature who is cool, dry, calm, articulate, independent, purposeful into a creature that is the opposite of these; to demonstrate to an animal which is pretending not to be an animal that it is an animal. But it seemed a good moment to keep quiet about all that. 'What would you say?' he asked after a short pause. 'A way of getting to know someone better than you can in any other way? That sort of thing?'

'Is that how you think of it?'

'Why so surprised? Don't a lot of people view it in that kind of way?'

'I guess so, it's just that somehow I shouldn't have expected . . .'

'What?'

'Roger, do you mind if I ask you a personal question?'

'Not in the very least. This is a fairly personal occasion.'

'Why are you so awful?'

'Yes, I used to ask myself that quite a lot. Not so much of late, however. Well, I think a frightful lot of it's tied up with being a snob, you know. Very angst-producing business, being a snob. No time to relax and take things easy. You have to be on duty all the time, as it were.'

'Oh, you know you're a snob, too?'

'As before, it's demonstrable.'

'I never knew you knew things like that about yourself.'

'You've never asked me.'

'No. Look, why aren't you awful now? Today you haven't been awful once.'

'I don't feel awful. I've no reason to feel awful. How could I be awful with you near me looking like that?' He leaned over and kissed her.

'What was that for?'

'For? You're looking surprised again.'

'You're noticing me.'

'Oh? Don't I usually?'

'I was expecting you to be really awful, a real son of a bitch, when I told you I'd loused up getting rid of Arthur . . .'

'I've explained about that.'

'. . . and I half thought, I more than half thought you'd

chew me out when I asked you about being awful just now. Why didn't you? I don't know how I had the courage to—'

'Because I really want you and I've got you. For an hour or so, anyway.'

'Oh, darling, do you really?'

'Of course, didn't I make that clear?'

'When?'

'Well, just now. You know.'

'Oh. Oh yes. Tell me more about being a snob. What sort of started you off on it?'

'That's easy, it was my father, no question about it. I'm not going to go into any of that Oedipus piffle but I really detested the bastard. He was a mean, vulgar, stupid little man who spent his evenings drinking beer and listening to variety programmes on the wireless and never noticed what he ate or wore or—'

'Take it easy, I suppose he'd come up the hard way and never—'

'Hard way, my God you should have seen it. Hard way indeed. No little sod ever had it easier. He didn't make the money. It was his father who'd done that. Magnificent old boy. Screwed a quarter of a million quid out of the peasantry in twenty years by flogging them bloody awful crockery and glassware as he called it. Learnt to drink claret and fish salmon and ride to hounds and adored it all. Fell down dead at eighty when he was out with his gun. No, my esteemed parent was a member of the upper classes, went to school at Charterhouse—Berkhamsted was good enough for me, he thought—and Captain of Boats at Magdalen, what? and then nothing. Doing anything was what the lower classes did. So was caring about anything. You mustn't have pictures in your house, because parvenus do that. So he sold my grandfather's Courbets and Dela-croixs and bought a racing car of some sort. He couldn't

drive it but he liked to know it was there. He didn't marry
a debutante—night-club owners and toy-balloon manu-
facturers do that. So he married the girl who answered
the telephone at his solicitors'. He saw quite a lot of them
because there were some things that had to be done and
he made them do them all.

'Perhaps I shouldn't say any of this,' he went on after a
moment, 'but I've got to blame someone for what I'm like,
haven't I?' Helene was gazing at him. He reached for the
top of the sheet that covered her and her hands went there
too for a moment, then released it. He pulled it away. There
was an interval before he continued : 'Will you come away
with me next weekend? To New York. Or anywhere you
like.'

She was silent for so long that he suspected sleep or the
feigning thereof, but finally her voice came from above his
head : 'Do you really want me to?'

'Of course I do.'

'You know, I think I might just manage it. I do believe
I might just swing it. I have an aunt in Cincinnati.'

'Have you really?'

'Well, I did ten years ago. There's Arthur, though.'

'So there is.'

'But then I've done a lot for Sue Green recently and she
felt bad about today. But then why can't Arthur go to
Cincinnati?'

'Your aunt's very eccentric. She doesn't like children.'

'Well, it's more she's a little feeble and frail. Be asking a
lot to expect her to put up with someone like Arthur.'

'Yes, it would, wouldn't it?'

'You never had any children, did you, Roger?'

'Darling, I wish you'd give these ghastly American
idioms a rest. The way you put it makes me sound ninety
years old or dead. No, I have never had any children. The
question has simply never arisen.'

'I guess not. All right, where can I call you when I've fixed things?'

'You've got my New York number.'

'Do I? You better give it to me again.'

'I've given it you before.'

'Never mind. Give it to me again.'

'Shall I?'

'Why don't you?'

'I suppose I could.'

'If you tried. Oh, Roger.'

'I love you, Helene.'

'We mustn't be too long.'

In the Bangs' bedroom next door the telephone rang, or rather set up its puny jangle. Helene sprang out of bed. 'I have to answer it.'

'Nonsense, my sweet, let it ring.'

'No, you never know, it's no good.'

Roger lay back and began to luxuriate slightly. By now it appeared to him that his behaviour to Helene over the last half-hour or so was a masterly feat of conscious policy, all of it successfully directed at getting her to come away with him in a week's time. He was too old a hand to exult prematurely—no roars of triumph until he bolted the door after them in the apartment bedroom—but conservative appraisal now put the chances at about sixty to forty in his favour, a miraculous recovery after the fifty-to-one-against assessable this morning. Hearing her voice on the telephone in the next room brought an unwelcome reminder of the small hours, and he even wondered momentarily whether he had done as much for her as Ernst had. But of course he must have done. The energy he had expended guaranteed that.

She reappeared now in the doorway, smoothing her hair back. In this attitude she looked as if she had recently grown a little in certain respects, which was remarkable. She said : 'It's for you.'

'For me? Who the devil wants me?'

'He wouldn't give his name. Just a friend, he said.'

'A friend? Well, that certainly narrows it down.'

'Don't be long.'

'You can rely on me.'

'I know.'

First carefully wrapping a sheet round himself, he went and picked up the telephone. 'Micheldene.'

'Mr. Micheldene?' The voice was American and so gave no clue.

'Micheldene.'

'Mr. Micheldene, I'm glad to have reached you. I called to inquire after your health.'

'Who are you?'

'Not your physical health, you understand, though I certainly trust that this continues satisfactory. I should like you to tell me how in your own personal view you rate your spiritual health as of this moment.'

Roger pulled his gaze away from the top of a nearby dressing-table on which, among pots and tubes and bottles of female stuff, he could see a man's necktie, neatly rolled up, and an empty plastic case of the kind used to transport electric razors. 'Whoever you are,' he said loudly, 'my spiritual health, like my genital and excretory health, is no concern of yours. Now just you—'

'Permit me to correct you, sir. As a priest of your Church your spiritual health is of peculiar and immediate moment to me. This is Father Colgate speaking. If you recall, the last time we made personal contact I expressed myself as having detected in you the infallible signs of a soul at variance with God. And now from the very tone of your voice over this telephone wire I find myself inescapably drawn toward the same conclusion. The unrest of a soul at variance with . . .'

Most of this passed Roger by. The reason he had not cut it short at once was that he had suddenly become very interested in the sound of a motor engine approaching the far side of the house. It stopped. There was the clumping noise of a door, followed by footsteps. He put the receiver down next to the telephone and ran out. In the passage there was a traditional moment when he and Helene, coming the other way, dodged and jostled like wrestlers, then he was in his own room snatching on clothes. The front-door buzzer buzzed, restoring perhaps a third of his calm, but he went on dressing while Helene's footsteps receded and paused. When he heard them returning unaccompanied he sat down on the bed in shirt, trousers and socks.

Helene came in wearing her housecoat and a pair of gold slippers and carrying a large fat envelope. 'It's for you,' she said. 'Special delivery. But don't—'

'What? Has everybody gone mad?'

'Don't open it now—wait till I have to go fetch Arthur.'

'What next? Chap driving a herd of cattle into the garden and saying they're for . . .'

He stopped speaking as he uncovered and recognised his lecture material and unfolded a note that read:

Dear Mr. Micheldene:

I took a look through some of this (hope you don't mind) and found it pretty interesting. It's quite an industry, isn't it? Not for me, though.

I guess I owe you an apology for not telling you ahead of time what I was going to do, but then that would have ruined the whole idea. I'm sure you understand.

Sincerely,

Irving Macher

PS: Watch out for Treatment no. 2!

'What's the matter?' Helene asked.

'Nothing. Excuse me a minute.'

He took a notebook from the breast pocket of his coat and went back to the telephone, which to his surprise was still talking with all its old authority.

'. . . process of education in remorse,' it said. 'But first, the freshman programme: horror, grief and fear. And there are no grades, my son. Here's one course of study where it takes no more than a heart honestly desiring to know—'

Roger spoke three words into the mouthpiece, of which two were 'the Pope,' rang off hard, looked through his notebook and dialled.

At his shoulder, Helene said: 'Who are you calling? What's this all about?'

Without turning or speaking he passed the contents of the envelope up to her. Then he said: 'Oh, good-afternoon. May I speak to Professor Parrish, please? Oh, could you tell me where I might reach him? Have you the number? Thank you, I'll try there.'

Helene tried several times to break in during this and while he re-dialled and he had to shake his head and make beating-off motions with his left arm to prevent her. Finally she got in with: 'This is this lecture of yours, right?'

'Yes yes, and Macher stole it. Fellow's a raving lunatic and I'm going to do something about... —Hallo, Budweiser College? The library, please.'

'But what can you do about it now, honey? Why does it have to be now? And anyway, wouldn't you do better to hold it until you've calmed down?'

He stared at her. 'I don't want to calm down. —Hallo, Professor Parrish, please. Well, could you go and see? Yes, of course.'

'Roger, look now.'

'Yes?'

'Isn't this what we called you being awful?'

'Yes, perhaps it is, but I'm afraid in the present situation that's neither here nor there.'

'The present situation? That's interesting. What is the present situation as you see it?'

'Helene dear, I'm not telling you to mind your own business, believe me, but you must recognise that this is a private matter between myself and this ... Jewish paranoiac. I'm sorry, but—'

'If it's between the two of you why are you bringing Parrish into it?'

'Kindly allow me to be the judge of—'

'Will you listen to me, Roger?'

'What is it?'

'We have about ten minutes at the outside before I have to go fetch Arthur. I shouldn't really have—'

'Hallo, yes? —All right, darling, see you later, then. —Are you sure? Bock 22? Would you put me back to the switchboard, then? Thank you.'

'At least you're convinced it wasn't Arthur now.'

'Just half a second, my dear, will you?—Switchboard? Bock 22, please.'

The bedroom door slammed. Roger made the beginnings of a movement towards it, then turned away and said into the telephone: 'English office? Professor Parrish, please. I don't care if you're the State Governor, I want to speak to Professor Parrish.'

It took several minutes for Roger to be convinced that he was not going to be able to do that. By the time he got back to his bedroom Helene and her clothes had gone, and almost at once he heard her drive away.

CHAPTER XII

'Before we get on to any of that, there is just one minor point I'd like to clear up, if I may.'

'I'll be glad to help in any way I can.'

'How did you get your hands on the stuff in the first place?'

'Oh, that was the most delightful part of it. I didn't have any ideas in advance, you understand, just a general policy. What happened, I went to hang up my hat in the cloakroom—'

'Your hat?'

'Yes. To be absolutely precise—since I own more than one hat—one of my hats. The hat I was wearing yesterday evening.'

'What sort of hat is it?'

'Well now, I guess you'd call it a dark olive-green in colour, made of some sort of felt, tapering somewhat from brim to crown but not too much, retailing at around—'

'Has it got bells and little bugles and brushes and stuff on it?'

'No, not this one, but I have one that does.'

'Why do you wear hats?'

'I like them. You like cigars, I like hats.'

'Yes, all right, go on with your story.'

'The first thing I saw in the cloakroom was this briefcase with these great golden initials on it. *R.H.St.J.W.M.*, or something of that order of complexity. An Englishman, I said to myself. And which Englishman? The Englishman who was going to give a lecture. I got all that at a

glance without having to go into the R. and the M. part
of it.'

'Brilliant.'

'No, I think that's overstating it—just alert, you know.
One thing, this *St.J.* interested me. Would that be Saint
John?'

At another time Roger would have confessed his inability
to see something, or have had to say he found himself at a
loss to comprehend something (or have given Macher a
left and right to the diaphragm). But with Suzanne Klein,
all snow-white hair-parting and vigorous black eyelashes
and scarlet linen dress, sitting on the other side of Macher
and evidently listening, that kind of stuff seemed ruled out.
Roger said airily, in the tone of one making a free gift of
half his attention : 'Well, yes, roughly, yes.'

'But isn't there something funny about the way you
pronounce it in England? Like Sunjohn?'

Roger articulated the name at him as if orally carving it
out of the air.

'Sinjurn...no. Sinjun. Rhymes with Honest Injun.
That's the way to remember it. Well, I shan't go wrong
in future, shall I?'

'Perhaps we could get on to the main point now,' Roger
said. He was not at all happy about the mood of chummy
collaboration which had spread across the discussion of
Macher's enormity, but information was needed and
punching time was still some hours off. 'Why did you steal
my lecture?'

'Temporarily remove it? It might be easier if I simply
explained my role.'

'I'm ready.'

'My role—in your life, that is—is to give you chances of
behaving naturally, that's to say not in prefabricated
sections, not out of some shooting script but off the cuff.
I told you some of this last evening, when you made your

show of tangling with that fool of a priest. I was interested to see that just afterward you got annoyed enough to remind me I'm a Jew. I liked that—it was a clumsy enough blow to show me you hadn't thought it out. And when you found your notes weren't there... Oh. You exceeded my best expectations. Like the first strong heartbeat after a man's pulled out of the water.'

'I think I understand you,' Roger said, nodding slowly. 'You're a divinely appointed scourge.'

For the first time since he had met him Macher showed some irritation. 'Not at all. You misunderstand me completely. This is what I do, not what I'm sent here to do. I'm your unsteadying influence, the flint in the road that gives your car a flat. No mission about it.'

'Our common destiny.'

'Wrong again, I'm sorry. It's what's happening, can't you see? It's how it is. If you say two people are made for each other you don't mean someone drew up specifications and built them, do you? Didn't you ever say to yourself, of course this had to happen this morning, this was all the situation needed, this girl I met last year was my undoing, this guy coming up just then with his offer was my salvation though I didn't know it then? If you can see this kind of thing afterward why can't you see it at the time?'

'I think because usually it isn't there to see,' Roger said as if choosing between half a dozen reasons. 'Most patterns are illusions based on insufficient evidence. An observer seeing red and black at roulette coming up alternately six times each might conclude he'd found a pattern, this was how it always went. Then red comes up twice running. End of pattern.'

'Intellectualist screen against phenomena,' Macher said, getting to his feet. 'I'll see you later.'

'I'll let you know when I've decided what my role is in your life.'

'Do that,' Macher yelled back over his shoulder, 'but
don't force it. Let it emerge.'

Macher had yelled not out of fury or sudden derange-
ment but out of necessity. The noise aboard the barge was
vast. In the bow a group of men in variegated orange or
violet shirts blew and banged with what must be most of
their strength at musical instruments. Roger had been told,
he could not imagine why, that they were all advertising
or insurance executives. The fifty-odd people on the benches
along the gunwale talked and laughed in a roar that fluc-
tuated little. The diesel engine aft kept up its shuddering
rumble, constantly sounding on the point of shearing its
bolts and flying through the side of the hull. Apart from
an overhead awning it was an open boat but sonically there
was a marked tunnel effect. It was a bring-your-own party
(with five dollars a head for the barge) and most people
seemed to have brought plenty of their own.

Roger's own was a bottle of whisky, half of it trans-
ferred to another bottle and both filled up with water. He
poured some into the paper cup held out to him by
Suzanne, who had moved up to fill Macher's place, and
who now said : 'Second quarter, both teams no score.'

As far as he could remember these were her first words
to him. Their relations had been confined to some vaguely
amatory quizzing on his part and a few go-thither looks on
hers. He soon decided what he would be with her. He
would be marvellous. He was always at his best, or least
bad, with new people, who could not have heard any of his
stories before; not from him, anyway. He said : 'What's it
like, being his girl friend?'

'I can't imagine. Oh, I'm not his girl friend. Not especially, that is. I go around with Prince Castlemaine too, and
Shumway and Hubler and that bunch? A girly girl, that's
me.'

'Oh, really?' This might mean several things short of

what he hoped it meant but surely not a preference for her own sex. 'Is Macher always like that?'

'Oh no, this is him being serious. He can be really wild. Likes to drink.'

'Does he mean all this stuff he talks?'

'Of course—he's terribly bright. Reads and thinks a lot.'

'Who does he read?'

'You know, these French writers, Sartre and Laclos?'

'I know. Look, Suzanne, about this little jest of his, one thing does strike me as slightly odd, two things rather. Anyway: why wasn't he afraid I'd report him to the College authorities, Maynard Parrish or someone?'

'You're not going to, are you?'

'Certainly not.' Roger could not now remember exactly why he had tried to telephone Parrish four hours earlier and did not try to do so. If he ever did it would appear to him that he had intended to express thanks for the dinner, exchange renewed commiserations about the un-delivered lecture and announce without explanation that the script had been recovered. 'But how could he know I wouldn't?'

'He didn't, but he figured you'd show up as too much of a fool if you did. In a way he was hoping you would. He's getting tired of Budweiser and to get expelled for a thing like this would be a great send-off for him and if it didn't come to that he'd still have a wow of a time over it. Couldn't lose, any way around.'

'Don't you think—this is the other thing—don't you think this approach of his to life, these pranks and so on, don't they strike you as just a little, unbalanced shall we say?'

'Hell no, Roger, he got it out of one of these French guys. Last year it was marijuana and mescalin. He doesn't do it all the time. Like once or twice a semester he gets kind of restless. They all do. John Page gets drunk and with Pitt Hubler it's finding a masseuse in Ammanford and

Irving . . . the last time he got restless he pretended to have
a brainstorm and started yelling and trying to strangle the
instructor who precepts in Jacobean Drama 311.'

'What happened?'

'The instructor hit him over the head with a glass paper-
weight and laid him out cold for nearly an hour.'

'I hope that was the reaction he was looking for.'

'Oh, better. He was delighted. Any lecture or anything
the guy gives now, Irving's there in the front row.'

'I'll have to make a frightfully special point of not doing what I wanted to do to him when I found out who'd
pinched my stuff or I'll have his undying devotion.'

'I think you're safe from that.'

Roger looked carefully round the barge, which was
patchily illuminated with half a dozen bare electric bulbs,
then carefully at Suzanne. 'Have some more,' he said, prof-
fering his current bottle.

'I'm fine.'

'I will, though, if I may . . . This boat's taking a long
time to get to where it's going.'

'You don't mind, do you?'

'No.' He looked carefully at her again. She had good
strong shoulders which she now moved to and fro slightly.
'Where is it going?'

'There's an island in the river where we'll picnic.'

'What, in this? It's as black as your hat already.'

'But not at all cold for the time of year. And there'll be
the lights from the boat and a couple of those stand-up
flashlights.'

'How big is this island?'

'I don't know, but someone said it had houses on it.'

'Sounds quite sizeable. Those lights won't reach far.'

'Are you afraid of the dark, Mr. Micheldene?'

'It's my natural element, Miss Klein.'

'That sounds rather fascinating.'

For the next twenty minutes or so Roger gave some hint of just how fascinating it was, or could be. Then he saw that the river was dividing and the tall silent Negro in a yachting-cap who was doing all the work—not every American tradition was suspect—started manipulating the engine and tiller. A short wooden jetty, half overgrown with weed, came into the lights. People started collecting their belongings together. Roger had his together already in a stout paper carrier: the two bottles of whisky, about a pound of sliced Virginia ham, some cold bacon, a hunk of Swiss cheese, two sorts of bread and a handful of apples. This was as much food as he had been able to find in the Bangs' larder. He had the problem of retaining contact with Suzanne without giving her anything to eat. There were other factors too. As the two of them stood up he put his free arm round her waist and said:

'We'll have to give things time to settle down. You see those two trees on their own with a light showing between them? No, over there.'

'Oh yes, just.'

'I'll see you somewhere round that spot in about twenty minutes.'

'All right. Here.'

She nudged him into a shadow and moved her face towards the side of his neck. Then she bit him sharply. The band had stopped and the engine was throttled right down, so that his hoot of pain and surprise, although he did his best to turn it into a laugh, rang out with some clarity. A lumberjacketed man who might quite well have been Fraschini turned and stared at him for an instant before being taken by a great hiccough that snapped his head back as if he had been uppercut.

'There's more where that came from,' Suzanne said.

'Half as much as that will easily see me through, thank you.'

The disembarkation was carried out efficiently and with the sense of common purpose characteristic of a task force which, though so far unopposed, expects to make first contact shortly. Once ashore, Roger attached himself unintimately to a group of people of whom he thought he recognised some, did some powerful eating and glanced about for Helene. There she was, her head and shoulders covered in yellowish light, with Macher and a couple of his friends. She nodded emphatically and laughed as Macher, forefinger jabbing, put some point.

At some later stage, Roger was aware, he was going to have to pass the time of night with Helene, perhaps a little more. Since fetching Arthur from his bear-hunt—Roger had been quite surprised to see him safe and sound after day-dreaming in such detail about an unusually active grizzly secured by a corroded chain—her behaviour had been definitely cold, cold enough to suggest the prudence of keeping out of her way for a few hours. He wondered what he was supposed to have done, apart, no doubt, from having failed to kiss her goodbye before she left for the zoo. He had honestly thought he had done enough fussing earlier. Really, they needed, or wanted, continuous propping up. The arrival of the fatal packet, true, had been unfortunately timed, but not by him. The basic trouble, obviously, was that events had given her a blunt reminder that the world was not all hers, that life must go on. None of them had ever learnt to face that simple fact.

Anyway, back to the present for the present. Roger crammed the last of the bread into his mouth and dunked it with so much whisky and water that a thin jet of it played from between his lips as he munched, but he craned his head forward and most of it missed his clothes. He got up and moved towards the two trees he had picked out. The air was soft and clear, with a faint breeze just perceptible as cool. Strong moonlight and irregular lamplight produced between them many tones and values of green and a medley of shadows. An occasional pale streak appeared on the river. Roger looked straight in front of him as he threaded his way between clumps of anonymous men and women towards his objective.

Just beyond the party area somebody approached him from the flank. He turned his head and stopped.

'Isn't this just great?' Mollie Atkins asked him. 'I'm sure there must be nicer places to be but I just don't seem to be able to think of any right now. Did you ever know a lovelier night than this?'

'It is very pleasant, certainly.'

She came up to him and peered into his face. 'You seem at a loss, friend. With my extensive knowledge of your habits and talents I find this totally uncharacteristic. And odd. However. This boat and picnic idea is kind of fun, isn't it? Very loosely organised, though. Do you realise it may take all of a half-hour to get all these folk rounded up and back in that boat, even if they start now? And they're not starting now. Do you realise that?'

Fifty yards away someone who might have been Suzanne Klein began moving in their general direction. Roger's mind jammed solid. 'I hadn't thought about it,' he said.

'Well, get started on thinking about it, old boy. Another point. Do you know this island at all?'

'Never been here before.'

'I know it like the back of my hand. Not that I know the back of my hand too well but I probably know it better than you do. Care to view some of its lesser-known beauties?'

The someone who might have been Suzanne had turned out to be Suzanne and she was now moving in their precise direction, purposefully. 'That would be fine,' Roger said, 'but hadn't we better leave it for a bit?'

Mollie turned at his nod. 'Oh. But what of it? Let's just get moving.'

'Well, I don't really think we can, do you? She's seen us.'

'What of it, for Christ's sake? Can't we go for a walk?'

'I wouldn't feel happy about it.'

'You British certainly care about what other people think, don't you? Or something. You must have made out on the boat like crazy. Hi, Suzanne.'

'Hi, Mollie.' Suzanne came up to them and stood smiling and looking from one to the other. She was shorter than Roger had realised. 'Well,' she said to him finally, 'here I am reporting for duty, captain, just like you said.'

Before she had finished speaking, Mollie began: 'You know, it's a very curious thing but I've suddenly been attacked by the most parching thirst anybody ever nearly died of. I just can't turn my mind to anything but that little old bottle down there at the camp-fire. So if you two children will excuse me I'll be on my way. Don't stay out too late. Bye for now.'

'That was a little obvious of me, I'm afraid,' Suzanne said.

'It had to be, you did it very well. Once we'd started to talk we could have gone on nattering here for an hour. Well, shall we go for that brief stroll we were talking about?'

'In a little while. How about something on account first?'

As he got hold of her Roger saw, over her shoulder, an abrupt shift in the pattern of illumination as somebody moved, or fell against, one of the standing lights. He could not tell whether or not this caused himself and Suzanne to become more visible, but he was able to make out a group of three or four people twenty yards off who might have been watching them. One of the group seemed to be wearing a white or mainly white dress, the sort of dress Helene had. Roger strained his eyes, trying to hold steady the unit temporarily formed by Suzanne's head and his own head, his pupils wheeling and plunging in time with its movements. Then the lights moved again, a shadow swung across and reduced the white dress to a floating blur, and in any case Roger found his attention urgently directed to matters nearer at hand. Suzanne's mouth had moved to somewhere near the base of his neck and now he felt it open suddenly. This gave him perhaps half a second's warning, not enough to avoid what was coming but enough to allow him to substitute a sort of hoarse falsetto moo for a full-dress scream when her sharp teeth dug deep through his shirt into one of the many ample folds of flesh at his shoulder.

As they sprang apart he lashed out at her with his fist, but she was alert and agile. From six feet away she said: 'Don't try it. I can move a lot faster than you. And you're outnumbered tonight.'

Roger relatively seldom hit a woman unless he was really angry or at least very drunk, and already his anger had begun to fade into puzzlement, even slight disquiet. 'What the hell are you up to?' he asked, rubbing his shoulder and wincing.

'Hey, I didn't bite you too hard, did I? I didn't mean to really hurt you. I'm sorry, it was the only thing I could think of to stop you quickly.'

'But why? I mean if you were going to stop me anyway why did you start me, back on that floating bloody madhouse? Eh?'

'I'm afraid I was just having fun in my own way. But Roger, it's really no worse than your way. My way causes fewer complications and it's over much quicker. And do you honestly think what you had in mind for me would have done anybody any good?'

'I suppose this is one of dear Irving's bright ideas?'

'Oh, only partly. You know, I don't think he's right about you never acting on impulse. We were arguing about this last night. You're certainly not big on forethought, are you? I saw the note Irving wrote you. Don't you ever listen when people warn you? I warned you.'

This friendly concern after a thoroughgoing act of physical and sexual hostility reminded Roger of Macher's polite readiness to explain and to debate. 'Kindly get out of here. Go away. Try somebody else. A woman for preference, eh? That's more your line, isn't it? Girly girl.'

'I really didn't want to hurt you. How awful. Let me take a look at it.'

Roger retreated. 'Take yourself off at once.'

'All right. I'm sorry.'

When she had gone, Roger took a pinch of Macouba from his teak snuff-box and then a lot more pinches until his nostrils were choked and burning. He would give it up now until he got back to England. He walked about slowly under the trees for ten minutes, blowing his nose into his yellow bandanna and trying to think. Could it be that he was never going to be able to revenge himself adequately on Macher? In the past, Roger had always found insults backed up by violence adequate to all his needs, but at the moment he could picture his enemy in a vat of boiling oil explaining the significance of the motive that had got him thrown into it. Roger realised too late that Suzanne might have been able and willing to help him with the problem. Curious girl, that.

He wandered back to his bottles, emptied one and started on the other. The party had split into a go-home faction and a stay-here faction. The latter was winning easily at the moment. Among it, sitting on the grass with their arms loosely round each other's shoulders, were Mollie Atkins and Joe Derlanger. Roger went over to them.

'This is a really nice atmosphere, isn't it?' Joe said, glaring up at Roger from under the peak of a baseball cap. 'Everybody friendly and no damn nonsense about who

with. Well, let's say a bit of damn nonsense but not too
much. Why don't you find yourself a girl, Rog?'

'He did,' Mollie said. 'At least I thought he did. Didn't
you?'

'I thought I had,' Roger said.

'Too bad.'

'Do you have a cigarette, Joe?' Mollie asked.

'Sure, doll.' His arm still round Mollie, Joe leant with
her some way over laterally while he felt vainly in a side
pocket with his free hand. Then, with narrowed lips, he
bore her in the opposite direction and reached across his
body to the other side pocket. 'I don't seem to... Wait a
minute.' He wrenched an unopened packet of cigarettes
from his top pocket and, again without freeing his arm,
set about tearing furiously at the wrapping with both sets
of fingernails. Mollie, her neck caught in the narrowing
crook of his elbow, began showing signs of distress. Joe got
to work with his teeth. 'This goddam *packaging*!' he said
in a muffled roar.

'Honey, if you'd just—'

'Jesus, you'd think they were trying to stop you getting
at the stuff.' He stabbed at the foot of the packet with his
forefinger and a couple of misshapen cigarettes climbed a
little way into view. 'Here.'

'I'm sorry, Joe, you don't have any with filters, do you?'

'No, I don't. Do you mind if I smoke one of these?'

'Not at all, if you think you can get it lit. —Roger, old
pal, do you think you can find me a filter cigarette? Then
I'll have absolutely everything I want, thank you kindly.'

Not very long afterwards people began to move back on
to the barge. Roger concentrated on getting a seat as far
away from the band as was consistent with avoiding Helene
and Suzanne and Mollie and Joe and Macher and Castlemaine and a few others. With a pull, or rather a violent
heave, of his drink inside him and a squat Havana in his

mouth, Roger settled himself like a good Christian to endure with patience and fortitude.

A mild commotion at the far end of the boat made him look up. There were shouts of jocose encouragement and a man called sharply: 'Hold it, Sam—one more to come.' The Negro at the controls immediately responded with engine and tiller. Roger, who had his back to the anchorage, saw a tall slim figure waving a bottle come at a fast run to the edge of the water and jump. It was Ernst. The gap was no more than four feet, but he slipped on taking off, missed the hands outstretched to him and landed awkwardly with one foot underneath him. The bottle flew out of his hand in a shallow parabola, to be caught almost at deck level by a white-haired man in a wine-and-tomato cubist shirt who hurled himself forward full length. This feat drew cheers.

'Pass completed.'

'Go, lion, go.'

'Always was a great little tackle.'

'Mow down that line of brown.'

'Wait a minute, fellows,' someone said. 'Seems Dr. Bang was shaken up on the play. Over here, Ernst.'

'That mad Viking.'

'Hey, Ernst, you all right?'

'What became of that bottle? Wouldn't want anything to happen to it after going back all that way.'

'I got it right here, Ernst, safe as the mail.'

'Well, come on, pour the guy some, he did a public service, didn't he?'

'Darling, are you sure you haven't hurt yourself?' Helene asked.

'I think perhaps I twisted something, but I'm all right.'

'He is now, anyway—right, Ernst?'

'Hell, who wouldn't be?'

CHAPTER XIII

A COUPLE OF HOURS later Roger found himself in a house that seemed to have no internal walls at all above waist-level. Rubber plants, cactuses, creepers, books, unexplained lumps of veined stone, Ivy League tobacco-jars, hedgehog clusters of black-painted iron spikes, paintings in two shades of black on miniature easels, bits of driftwood that might be held to resemble some creature or man-made object, purple or brown glass bottles evidently specially made but not for the storage of fluids lay on jagged slate shelves, between vertical dividers of cherry and stripped pine, next to fluted white pillars dashed with pink mottling. Good place for a gun-fight, Roger decided as he helped himself to a drink out of a stone barrel bracketed to the wall in one corner. Or any sort of fight, really.

Carloads of people arrived at longish intervals. Some had stopped to buy pizza on the way; others said the house was hard to find or said nothing at all. Roger was standing at the top of a few marble steps near a Moorish doorway outlined in fluorescent lighting when Strode Atkins came in. He was soaking wet from crown to toe and was smoking a cigarette. He nodded amiably to Roger. 'Seem to have been in the river,' he said.

'So I see. Was it cold?'

'I think so. Couldn't tell you for sure . . . You're British, aren't you?'

'Yes, I am. My name's Micheldene.'

'I'm pretty sure we've . . . some place . . .'

'Yes, we have. At the Derlangers' last Sunday night. And

just to put your mind at rest we've been into Tommy
Atkins and oat and aboat and why do we hate you. And
you being a horrible Anglophile.'

Atkins's face lit up slowly. 'So we did,' he said in wonder. 'Hey, so we did at that. I remember now. Well, what
do you know? You're my old friend Mitch Dean. How you
making out, Mitch old man? How do you like this
country?'

'As well as I ever did.'

'Great. Hey . . .' Atkins stood and dripped for a time
while his face darkened as slowly and thoroughly as it had
brightened. 'Hey, there was something else that evening,
wasn't there?'

'Strode? Strode, come along up and get some dry clothes
on.'

'Be with you in a minute, Al. Just want to settle a point
with my old friend Mitch here. —Yeah, there was something else . . . What the hell was it?' After a pause which
Roger used to get his feet into a favourable position, Atkins
seemed to come to a decision. He held out his hand and
looked Roger in the eye. 'Mitch, old son, I'd like to tell
you I'm sorry and I'd like for you to shake my hand to
show me you bear no ill-will.'

Roger stared. 'Sorry? What about?'

'Well now, as to that, Mitch, you rather have me. I
don't seem to recall exactly what about. But this much
I do know. There was some kind of . . . unpleasantness
in which you and I were involved.'

'What of it?'

'This of it, Mitch. This of it. I make a rule that if I'm
involved in any . . . unpleasantness then I apologise afterward. It's nearly always been my fault anyway and if it
wasn't, what the hell? Better somebody apologises than nobody, huh? Are you going to shake?'

Roger shook and Atkins clapped him on the back.

'That's my boy,' he said approximately. 'All friends now. Be seeing you around.'

He made a good if slow job of the stairs and squelched off across the rugs and tiles and wood blocks to his host's side without once taking a wrong turning. Roger found his glass was empty.

He was refilling it for the second time when Nigel Pargeter came up to him. When he saw who it was Roger threw up mentally. Pargeter, for God's sake. What did the fellow think he was doing, hanging about the place in this fashion? Who had asked him along and how had he presumed to accept? Pargeter—it was dreadful to have to face the fact of his existence. The notion of the universe as the handiwork of the Almighty received a severe check at Pargeter. Nevertheless Roger greeted him effusively. There was a fist-fodder air about Pargeter that was rather appealing. 'Hallo, Pargeter, stands England where she did?'

The man ignored this and looked busily about for some seconds. This and the way he spoke suggested that he had approached Roger because he knew Roger and Roger was on his own rather than because Roger was Roger. He said to Roger: 'I wonder if you could give me a hand. There's a bit of trouble going on outside and I thought perhaps you might give me a hand.'

'What sort of trouble?'

'Bit of trouble with Joe Derlanger.'

Roger followed Pargeter through what was no doubt the hallway alcove or the lobby area to the front door. This had worm-holes in it that might have been put there with red-hot knitting needles but was otherwise unremarkable. 'What sort of trouble?'

'He's acting up. Seems to have got himself into a bit of a state.'

'Fighting anyone?'

'Not yet.'

As they left the porch there was the clanging boom of a hard object striking metal. Then Roger saw Joe, brightly lit by powerful bulbs in fisherman's lanterns hung aloft on poles, take a pace forward and very single-mindedly kick the door of a car: his own, as it proved. The booming noise was repeated. Small dents in the door and elsewhere testified to earlier kicks. Five yards from him Grace Derlanger stood, her shoulders bowed and her hands over her face. Pargeter went up and put his arm round her. 'Please don't, Joe honey,' she called. 'Please don't. Take me home. I'm so tired.'

'Not till I'm good and ready,' Joe said. He sounded preoccupied. 'I'll finish this and then I'll go call a taxi.' Rubbing his chin and slowly shaking his head in a dissatisfied way, he contemplated the car for a few moments, then turned decisively and strode off round the side of the house.

Roger joined Grace and Pargeter. 'What's this all in aid of?' he asked.

'It's just the way he gets sometimes,' Grace said, swallowing. 'I don't have any idea what causes it or what he gets out of it. When I ask him tomorrow he'll say he doesn't remember.'

'Come on inside, Grace,' Pargeter said. 'Let me take you inside and give you a drink. You won't do any good here. He might stop if you went inside.'

'No, I have to stay and see it. It makes no difference whether I'm here or not—he isn't aiming it at me.'

'Perhaps he's got fed up and gone indoors himself,' Roger said.

'He'll be back. He hasn't finished yet. He won't stop until he's wrecked it.'

'Come inside and have a drink, Grace,' Pargeter said.

'I'll stay, thank you, Nigel. You go in. Oh, here he is.'

Joe came into view again, carrying what looked like an iron bar. He swung it accurately at the near headlamp and

there was a dull explosive sound without any hint of
breaking glass. 'This is more like it,' he said, moving over
to the other headlamp.

Roger felt some concern. He went and stood in front
of Joe and said: 'This is a bit of a bloody waste of time,
isn't it, Joe?'

'Out of the way, Roger, please.' Joe's tone held no
menace. He might have been asking his opponent to leave
him an unimpeded shot at a two-yard golf putt. 'Just move
aside, will you?'

'This is going to cost you a few quid, Joe. As it is. Plus
a lot of embarrassing explanation. I'd call it a day if I
were you. I'm saying this as a friend.'

'The sooner you move aside the sooner I'll be through.
This is my car and I can do what I like with it. Right now
I want to beat it up some.'

Pargeter came and stood at Roger's side. 'Why not give
it a rest, Joe?'

'Look, I know you guys mean well but all you're doing
is hold me up, do you understand? Just pipe down and
let me get the job done. Won't take more than a minute
or two.'

'Wouldn't she start, or what?' Pargeter asked.

'It isn't the car. Now quit standing in the light, will
you please?'

Roger and Pargeter went back to Grace. Joe knocked out
the surviving headlamp and stood considering for a time.
Then he broke the windscreen. This time the sound of
shattering glass was abundant. Roger left Pargeter with
Grace and turned away towards the house. His feelings of
concern had ebbed. It would have been agreeable to stop
Joe but the matter was not of great importance. At the
same time Roger was dissatisfied. More than once, he
seemed to remember, he had been near the point of telling
Joe something about Helene and even, conceivably, asking

his advice. But he realised now that he would not have known how to set about it. It was impossible to talk to them about anything more personal than baseball without having been in the same class at Yale or in Phi Upsilon Kappa with them.

Somebody was standing in the shadowed porch when he entered it. Repeated encounters with Mollie Atkins now ensured almost immediate recognition of her. This was she. She was standing on one foot and swaying slightly to and from the door-post and she had a drink in her hand. She held this out to him without speaking: Roger took it and drank it.

'Thank you very much.' He took a step nearer the door, but the steady surging noise of people in the house gave Joe's spasmodic break-it-yourself efforts a kind of rural charm. Except for the reluctant sound of falling glass there seemed to be quite a lot of space and silence. Roger turned to Mollie and took her arm. 'How about a little fresh air,' he declared.

Mollie hopped and then lurched against him and her lengthy necklace of what looked like fossilised birds' eggs (or pottery imitations of this nasty idea) swung painfully against his midriff.

'For heaven's sake, can't you so much as walk?'

'If you mean am I smashed the answer is yes. But that's not the trouble.' She took another—from Roger's point of view—painful hop. 'I have the standard number of feet but I don't have the shoes to match: I was coming out to look for it. Hang on a minute.' She bent and came up with a high-heeled sandal.

'Well, if you left the other one in Joe's car I doubt if it would be wearable by now.'

With the pedantry he recognised wearily as belonging to her state, she said: 'I didn't leave it in Joe's car, because

that was not the way I came to this house. Grace came
here in Joe's car, with Joe; I came here in Al's car, with
Al.'

There was a by now more distant rupturing crash from
Joe's direction. Roger had steered them well round the
corner of the house, with some difficulty. Mollie need not,
he reflected, be as capable as all that, but how capable was
that? Women had tiresome habits when drunk, becoming
either irritatingly dependent or unreasonably aggressive.
In fact, without a few decent inhibitions they could be a
confounded nuisance. But Mollie interrupted this:

'At least he only does it to things. He's quite patient and
kind with people really. He blew up a water-heater one
time and it made more of a bang than he expected and he
was terrified someone might have gotten hurt.'

'What are you talking about?' He had managed to back
her up against a fairly substantial tree, and saw no need for
her to talk at all, about anything.

'About Joe. He's worth our weight in gold. And with
you counted in, old boy, that's quite some weight. We
haven't done too well tonight, have we? Why do you think
that is?'

'But he's been breaking up his car.'

'I know it. I'm talking about it. You think it's childish
of him, don't you? You think it would be more adult if
he'd gotten hold of me or someone and had some fun at
their expense, don't you?'

'Look, if you're going to talk like that—'

She had seized his jacket and the shirt inside it and some
of his arms inside that and held him in a surprisingly firm
grip. 'Just relax, honey...' To his slight astonishment she
was hauling, or levering, him on to the ground, and he had
just enough time to decide that he would prefer to be sitting
down before he did so. American women seemed entirely

without finesse. He preferred frank submission to frank pursuit except, theoretically, from the kind of woman who frankly made no move of any kind in his direction.

'...comes a time when you can't get exactly what you want...'

What was she droning on about? Suzanne Klein's attentions were probably a result of the twofold insecurity of being Jewish and American (and the consequent aggression). Her youth was only a temporary advantage beside such fundamental handicaps.

'...so much better if people like us made the most of what's available...'

She was leaning against him rather for her own comfort than to give him pleasure, and his mounting resentment focused momentarily on being treated as an out-of-doors sofa. All this dragging and pawing him about was clearly the consequence of her being a middle-aged nymphomaniac, and not a particularly attractive one at that. If Helene had had the common courtesy to be decently polite to him, let alone nice, none of the evening's physical indignities would have taken place. After all he was her *guest*, wasn't he?

Mollie had put a hot dry hand to his face. '...should make people in our position kinder to each other? What do you say, Rog?'

He took a deep breath to ensure rapidity of fire. 'I fail to see any similarity in our positions. I have, fortunately for you, been taking almost no notice of your nonsense. But considering your time of life I would advise you to conduct yourself with a little more dignity. Most men don't enjoy drunken women after a certain age making passes at them. You have a perfectly good husband. I suggest you pay a little more attention to him.'

He had succeeded in shaking off her hand, and with some difficulty—there was nothing to help him—had risen to his feet. There was a moment of complete silence during which he realised that all sounds of Joe and his car had stopped. Getting up had somehow interfered with what should have been an unanswerable exit line. She lay exactly as she had collapsed when he removed his support: on her back, staring up at him without moving. Then she said:

'Beat it, Mr. Englishman. I want to be alone with the memory of your old-world courtesy. So beat it.'

Her voice was quiet and flat, but higher in pitch than usual. Roger stood there a moment experiencing, unusually for him, a mixture of feelings. One of them resembled agitation.

He hurried into the house and went in search of the man Al who seemed to own it. Al was standing talking to a group that included Helene, Suzanne, Macher, and a couple of Macher's followers. Ernst was also listening from a plush-covered armchair, one leg out in front of him on a footstool of rawhide and tubular steel. Once or twice he moved his foot experimentally.

'So the guy wakes up on the edge of the turnpike,' Al said, 'a few feet away from what's left of his car, and he decides he must have been knocked crazy, because bending over him there's a one-eyed Negro, a man-sized rabbit and an Apache with all the feathers and paint and junk. He figures he's strayed into *The Wizard of Oz* or somewhere. Then the Indian says to him in a Boston accent: "I think you're all right but I'll have to examine you further. Now don't worry about a thing—I'm a doctor," and the guy screams: "Keep your hands off me, you savage," oh, and there's a lot more before he realises it's Hallowe'en and these are three guys on their way to a—'

'Excuse me,' Roger got in finally, 'but have you a telephone directory? Something rather urgent has come up.'

'Sure, you just come with me,' Al said, taking him by

the arm and steering him round various corners. 'Nothing bad, I hope? Anything I can do to help?'

'Thank you, I can manage.' Roger soon found the address he wanted and was looking for a taxi number when Helene appeared.

'What's the matter, Roger? Are you sick?'

'No. There's somebody I must see, that's all.'

'Can't you call them? It's kind of late to go visiting. Who is it?'

'No, I have to see them in person...Here we are: Keeley's Taxi Hire.'

'Keeley never comes out after midnight. Where do you want to go? How far?'

'It's in the town somewhere. I don't know how far that is.'

'Not more than five minutes. How long will it take you when you get there?'

'I don't know. A quarter of an hour. Twenty minutes perhaps.'

'I'll drive you and I'll bring you back if you're not too long. I have to get Ernst home some time.'

'Would you, Helene?'

'Sure. Who is it you're going to see?'

'I'll tell you later. It's nobody you know. I want to go to the lavatory first.'

'I'll meet you outside.'

In the bathroom, which had walls all the way up to the ceiling, Roger found he was not actually going to be sick. He sat on the closed lid of the w.c., which resembled apricot marble, and kept quite still for a minute or two. Then he drank some water and splashed more of it over his face and scalp.

Outside the porch the Bangs' green-and-brown station wagon was waiting for him. He got in beside Helene and they moved off. As they passed Joe's car, which someone had pushed half off the drive, a voice said interestedly from the back seat: 'Somebody seems to have been expressing himself there.'

Roger shut his eyes. He asked very slowly: 'What is that little shit doing in this car?'

'I brought Irving along to keep me company while you're doing whatever it is you're going to do. It's not any fun to be a girl on your own in the middle of town at this time of night.'

'Good God, woman, you'll be in the car, won't you? You're not expecting them to come at you with crowbars, are you?'

'Oh, that's not the point.'

'Isn't it? Isn't it the point? You're all the same. Got to be feather-bloody-bedded all the time. Being looked after— i.e. exacting unreasonable concessions. Being wanted. Getting more than your fair share of attention at all times.'

'Look, Roger, I know you're stoned, but if you go on this way you're going to say something you'll be sorry for.'

'You're probably quite right, my dear. Trouble is those are the only things I really enjoy saying.'

Macher's laugh came from behind Roger. 'I have to admit your method does pay off now and then, Mr. Micheldene. Compared with mine it stinks in general but there are a few things it can do and mine can't.'

'We can do without your puny little comments, Macher. Going back to where we were...A woman tries to get a man into a position in which he—'

Helene trod on the brake so abruptly that Roger's forehead brushed the windscreen. 'How would you like to walk the rest of the way?' she asked him.

'Have a care, will you?...I'm sorry. I really am sorry. I really hardly knew what I was saying,' Roger said truthfully. 'I'm a bit upset. I didn't mean it. I know I was being awful. I couldn't help it. Please forgive me.' He put his hand on her wrist.

She let his hand stay there for a quarter of a minute while nobody spoke or moved. Then she said quietly: 'All right, but no more cracks,' and drove off.

The rest of the trip passed in silence. Roger got out into a deserted street with terraced three-storied houses and a few shops in it. He went up to one of the houses and rang the bell. When nothing had happened after a minute he started battering on the door and bawling:

'Come down here. Come down at once, you long-frocked clown. I know you're in there. No use trying to hide from me. Let me in this instant, you spiritual dentist. Come and do what you're paid to do, curse you. Confess me. Confess me. If you're not down here in one minute I'll set the bishop on to you. Shop.'

Some neighbouring lights went on in upstairs rooms and a couple of windows were raised. A voice called in reasoned protest. Then the door in front of Roger opened and a tall stout Negro in white pyjamas confronted him. 'What can I do for you?'

'Let me pass, please.'

'Be so good as to state your business.'

'Where's your boss?'

'I am the boss here. This is my house. What is your business?'

'Where's Colgate?'

'My name is Miller. There is no Colgate here, I assure you.'

'Must be. Priest chap. Dog-collar.'

'Ah, now I believe I can help you. A young man in holy orders lives in one of the houses across the street. Number 19. No doubt he is the object of your search.'

'Isn't this number 19?'

'No, number 19 is across the street.'

'Thanks.'

'Good-night.'

A little later Roger was sitting in a sitting-room full of potted palms and tanks of fish and Father Colgate, wearing a shiny yellow dressing-gown, was saying to him :

'In your present condition, physical, emotional and spiritual, I should not be justified in agreeing to hear your confession, sir. You appear to be actuated by selfish motives, motives in which resentment plays a large part. As I see it, your pride has been hurt and you wish me to restore it. Now this is no part of the function of a—'

'Rubbish, my pride's in perfectly good order. And as for resentment, any fool could see I've got a lot of that and no wonder. Do you understand the system you're helping to perpetuate, Father? It's not the unreasonableness of it I'm attacking. Not at the moment, anyway. It's the barbaric injustice of expecting people who are defenceless against—'

'Now just hold it there—take it easy, my son. What this woman said to you appears to have disturbed you somewhat, and evidently the question of sexual behaviour was raised, but other than that I'm unclear as to what passed between you. Could you fill me in on a little detail, please?'

'Well, she said . . . Never mind what she said. That's neither here nor there. The point was it set me thinking about what we're all up against. Now patently we're up against a very great deal but it doesn't take much nous to see—'

'Pardon me one moment, sir, but this word . . . nous? I don't—'

'Oh, do forgive me, I forgot I was in America. What is it, five schools in the whole country still teaching Greek? Nous : intelligence, penetration, reasoning faculty.'

'Proceed.'

'Thank you, I mean to. The . . . Yes. The people I've got it in for are you and your lot. Making a good living out of

telling the rest of us we put all the bad things there ourselves. Lust. Yes, I distinctly remember women being in-
vented. Same as drink. Father, I am a dipsomaniac. Well,
don't blame me, my son—distillation wasn't referred to
anywhere on those bloody tablets at Mount Sinai. You did
that. Father, I am a drug addict. You can't say I didn't
warn you, my son. I told you not to touch that apple.
Father, I suffer from—'

'See here, my son, why don't you just go home and get
some sleep and come back and have a little talk when
you're less confused, huh? Why don't you?'

'I'll confuse you, you bead-telling toad. I wouldn't take
your absolution if you begged me. Try absolving yourself
from the disgrace of abetting a disgrace. And stop telling
me what to do, you silly little man.'

Roger picked up Father Colgate and walked with him
to the most capacious of the fish-tanks and held his face
just above the surface, which was shifting minutely with
the inflow and outflow system. Fish recognisable as gold-
fish, others with vertical stripes and moronic startled faces,
scurried into the bottom corners. '*Auctoritate mihi com-
missa*,' Roger intoned, '*ego te condemno in nomine Patris*,'
—he immersed Colgate's nose and mouth—'*et Filii*,'—
Colgate went in up to the hairline—'*et Spiritus Sancti*'—
head and neck. Displaced water slopped over the sides.
Roger stirred the tank vaguely with Colgate for a moment,
then took him away and dropped him on to a sofa. Colgate
coughed and gasped. 'Good-night, Father, and thank you.
You've been a great help. Pray for me.'

CHAPTER XIV

'AND BY NATURE she's such a considerate woman,' Ernst said. He pressed his lips together and shifted his plaster-covered foot into a new position on the oak-backed sofa. 'What a confounded nuisance this thing is. Wouldn't you say, Roger, that she's a considerate woman?'

'Certainly I would.'

'I'm sure she's shown herself considerate in all her dealings with you. It does seem out of character, doesn't it? No note or anything like that. But she didn't go off on impulse. A great delivery of groceries arrived this afternoon, more than enough to see Arthur and myself through the weekend. And Sue Green dropped by just before you arrived and said she understood Helene was away for a couple of days and could she do anything. So there was premeditation—silly word. I think quite likely I'll get a letter tomorrow which will explain a good deal, but... It's so unlike her, don't you agree?'

'Most emphatically I agree.' Roger tried to put on the expression of a practised and sincere fact-gatherer. 'Has she ever done this kind of thing before?'

'Never—that's what admittedly alarms me rather. Never spent more than a couple of hours out of my company that weren't accounted for. And now it's... getting on for twelve. A significant difference. She probably left soon after I did this morning. It was Mary Selby's turn to fetch the kids from school and she gave Arthur tea. I don't know whether that was prearranged. I haven't liked to ask.'

'Has she gone to her parents, do you suppose?'

'No, I talked to her mother on the telephone last night. Had the devil of a job convincing the old girl that there was nothing up. No, it's fairly obvious what's happened to her. She's with a man.'

'Oh, do you really think so?' Whether or not Ernst really thought so, Roger did. He had thought so fairly continuously from the moment, three hours ago, when Ernst had rung him up in New York and told him of Helene's disappearance. And thinking so had been disagreeable to Roger. Although he had felt far from good that morning when Helene's letter had reached him, saying that Ernst had evidently broken a small bone in falling and found it painful to move and so she had to be with him and so the weekend trip was off, Roger had not really been surprised. It just showed up an inherent snag about all dealings with women: that they involved women. Ernst's revelation that his foot was only a selective curb on Helene's activities was far harder to assimilate. So was the observed fact that the foot made its owner's movements laborious rather than painful. And so was the thought of who Helene had gone off with.

Ernst brought this last point up now by saying: 'Who do you think Helene has gone off with?'

'You mean you know? I shouldn't have thought—'

'I'm asking your opinion. It's a rather expert opinion in this case. You know, Roger, I'm really quite surprised this hasn't come up before. I married a very attractive woman. I don't have to tell you that for a good deal of the time there's been some male or other hanging about. I don't resent that and it's never been a difficulty between us. And if she chooses to spend the afternoon in bed with an occasional one of these males then I regard this as her affair.'

'Oh, but surely, I'd have thought she was completely—'

'Roger, please.' Ernst smiled in a way that made Roger's

own smile of cordial disbelief turn stiff on his face. 'I know what Helene does without her having to tell me. It's a part of being married, you know—well of course you do know (please forgive me) as a married man yourself. Now I must admit that I don't altogether understand exactly why she does this with the males. Agreed, she's a very passionate girl. And we all have our natural curiosity, especially in sexual matters. And then again Helene's also a very sympathetic girl. It's a funny thing, but the males she chooses are always... Well, let's just say that none of them has ever represented the slightest threat to the long-term stability of our married life. Until now. This is a different behaviour-pattern altogether. Now I do feel threatened, I must confess. Otherwise I wouldn't have dreamt of bothering you with my troubles in this way. It was very good of you to drop everything and come down here so promptly. But now you're here I must ask your opinion. Who in your view is the likeliest candidate? Surely you must have an idea.'

'Irving Macher,' Roger said.

'Exactly what I said myself. He's been round here a couple of evenings this week. I didn't discourage him because he's an intelligent and amusing young fellow and I didn't think he was Helene's type at all. I still don't, in a way. It's curious... You know, Roger, when I first realised she'd gone I thought for the moment that you might be the culprit. But then I decided you couldn't be. Well, we'll just have to be patient, I suppose. I've got a feeling we'll probably hear some news in the morning. Excuse me just a minute, I'll make sure Arthur doesn't want something.' He pushed himself to his feet and limped slowly out of the room.

Roger sat and tried to think. He found it difficult. He was still emotionally fatigued by having had to suppress his violent curiosity—Ernst had given no details whatever over the telephone—for over an hour after arriving. As might easily have been predicted, Arthur had still been conspicuously up and incessantly about, asking questions about Mommy's aunt in Cincinnati, whether Mommy had gone there in a jet plane, and very much more. It was no wonder that people were so horrible when they started life as children.

But the effects of Arthur's ambience—his usual conversational shout was even now audible off stage at short intervals—were less distracting than thoughts of Helene. Every consideration demanded that it should be Macher who got thought about, plotted against, circumvented, punished. Yet each time Roger started from this point he ended up with some memory of Helene. No doubt it would be better when he was clear of the house.

Ernst came back, his plaster cast clopping irregularly on the tiled floor. 'Let's have another drink, Roger. I feel like it this evening. Let's get high together, shall we?'

'I'd like to, but unfortunately I only have time for one. I must be getting back to New York soon. There's a train—'

'Oh, but why must you go? I'd hoped you'd do the family-friend act and stay and hold my hand. I'd hoped you might stay the night.'

'I'm afraid that's quite out of the question. As it is I shan't be indoors until well after eleven and I'm off to New Haven first thing in the morning. It's a pity, it would have been nice.'

'Oh well, help yourself to one for the road, then. And you might top me up while you're about it.'

Roger did this and stood gazing into his drink. He said thoughtfully: 'I wonder where they've gone.'

'Somewhere in New York, undoubtedly. They'd get right out of this area and Helene loves New York. She's always on to me to take her there so that she can hear some authentic jazz. She says that jazz in Scandinavia is quite interesting as far as it goes but it isn't authentic. I don't understand these matters myself, I must confess.'

'Neither do I, I'm happy to say. Does she know New York well?'

'She's never lived there.'

'Got any friends in the place?'

'None that I know of. Oh, they'll have slipped into some hotel somewhere.'

'Then you've really no idea where they'd be?'

'No, I don't, and even if I . . .' Ernst broke off, smiling and frowning. 'Infectious, isn't it, don't you find?'

'What is?'

'*Do* and *don't* for British *have* and *haven't*. It's as if Americans regarded having as an activity whereas Englishmen regard it as a state, a condition. I connect this with the frequent American preference for *this* where British usage would favour *that*—*who is this?* on the telephone, for instance, as opposed to *who is that?* Thus where an American typically says *I do this*, showing concern with an activity related to an object that is immediately present, an Englishman typically says *I have that*, showing concern with a condition that need be none of his making and is related to an object that may be at a distance and in the past. Americans pursue the dollar; the British had an empire. Fascinating to see the underlying assumptions and goals of a culture laid bare in its idiom. Fascinating, but not surprising. Language is before anything else the great social instrument.'

'Yes,' Roger said. 'I'd better get hold of a taxi or I shall miss my train.'

He took the taxi not to the station but to the main entrance of Budweiser College. In parody of an Oxford porter's lodge there lounged a man dressed as a policeman. 'Pilsener 33,' he said in answer to Roger's question. 'Block at the end of the first square.'

The first square was ivy-covered Gothic. *A.D. MCMXXIX*, a plaque on a heavily buttressed and sporadically gargoyled chapel proclaimed. Before he found the right staircase Roger glanced through an arch got up like one of the gates at Caius, Cambridge and caught sight of a great glass-and-concrete box that might have been lifted straight out of the business quarter of Manhattan. Oh, they made strides here.

There was nobody on the far side of the door marked *I. A. MACHER*. After some effort of memory Roger tried *P. M. CASTLEMAINE, T. SHUMWAY JR* and *P. C. HUBLER*, but with no better result. Or very little better. Two adjacent walls of the last room were largely covered with rectangles of black cardboard. On one of these were half a dozen photographs of men of at least two races blowing into what Roger assumed were saxophones of various sorts; on the other were perhaps five hundred photographs of girls. Roger looked at them uneasily. He was for this and against it. What right had P. C. Hubler to interest himself in this field? Young men these days seemed to think it was all right for them to start on girls whenever they felt like it, as if they were just like anybody else.

As Roger was about to leave another policeman passed the entrance and saw him. 'Hey, what you nosing around in there for,' the man said, coming up and carefully looking Roger over from head to toe, 'sir?'

'I'm looking for Mr. Castlemaine or—'

'Well, you want to try his room.'

'I've tried his room. He isn't there.'

'Oh, he isn't? Well, he'll probably be over at the pep rally right now. That's where a lot of them went. Still be going on, I guess. That's where he most likely is. Unless of course he's a grind. Is he a grind?'

'Look . . . In the first place what is this pep rally?'

'For the big game tomorrow. The Rheingold game, you

know? Over at Dunkles Arch. You know, it's kind of like
a demonstration. Listen, you can hear them now.' A hundred yards away there was cheering and shouts and an
explosion. 'That's them. That's them firing the cannon.'

'Thank you, I think I can find them.'

'Wait a minute, you sure Castlemaine isn't a grind?
Because if he's a grind he won't be there, he'll be—'

'What is a grind?'

'A grind,' the other said very slowly, 'is a young man
who is very interested in reading his books. He is so interested in reading his books that he spends a great amount of
time in the library. He does not go to pep rallies or other
things like this because he is too interested in—'

'Thank you, thank you. Tell me, why are there all these
policemen about the college? Are people expecting some
sort of trouble?'

'No more than usual. And I'm not a policeman, not a
regular policeman. I just dress like one. I'm a proctor.'

'A *proctor*?' Roger thought of the fine-featured, ascetic
dons (dismissible in most other contexts as pompous
boobies) who in gown and bands upheld the dignity of this
ancient office (antique tomfoolery) in the streets of his
mother university.

'Yeah, and don't upset yourself, mister, I didn't invent
the name, it's just what the fellows who pay me call me.
You like me to get it changed?'

Dunkles Arch and its environs were lit by chains of
electric bulbs hung from windows and, now and then, by
magnesium flares. It was enough to enable Roger to pick
out any of Macher's followers who might be among the
several hundred people present. Roger moved from group
to group, trying to shut his ears to the tumult. An incom-
prehensible chant was in progress to start with, conducted
by a number of persons with megaphones in their hands
who capered rhythmically about on the steps below the

arch. Among them was somebody entirely encased in the
skin of a bear. The cannon went off. A song was sung to
the accompaniment of a brass band. Over a public-address
system a man called Coach Oxenreider was introduced and
said what he thought support meant. Roger failed to
understand his drift. Somebody else was introduced and
introduced somebody else. The first one said: '...star right
guard...not very bright but sure can play football...fine
game against Schlitz and the Press thought so too...came
all the way from Portland, Maine to play football for
Budweiser...on the bench most of last fall and already...'
The second one said: '...soon as I saw a leg I broke it.'

A spirit of definite objection had been gathering in
Roger. Now, as the hollow voices went on and the immense
shadows on the surrounding walls shifted violently with
small resettings of the spotlights, he felt a faint stirring of
bewilderment. At almost the same time he caught sight of
Castlemaine standing with another young man and two
girls and went over to him. 'Can I have a word with you?'

'Why, it's Mr. Micheldene. Good-evening, sir, and what
brings you—?'

'This is private.' Roger moved a couple of yards off and
Castlemaine, with a wondering air, followed. 'Now.
Where's Irving Macher?'

'I can't answer that with any certainty, not having seen
him all day, but no doubt he's somewhere around the—'

'That will do. Where is he?'

'Mr. Micheldene, I do believe you're agitated. I thought
the British were never agitated.'

'That will *do*, Castlemaine. I may say that if I fail to
obtain any satisfaction from you I shall go straight to
Professor Parrish and tell him I have reason to believe that
Macher is not in college. Perhaps Parrish is the wrong man
to go to and I know nothing of the rules of this bizarre
establishment, but I imagine I could make an adequate

amount of—' Roger winced as the cannon fired again.
'...of trouble for Macher if I act as I have described.
Right. Where is he?'

Castlemaine peered at Roger. 'That's a most impressive
demonstration of sportsmanship and fair play, so much so
that I'll gladly tell you all I know. Irving is in New York
City, I don't know where, but it's some place belonging to
a friend of his whose name I don't know. That should
narrow it down for you, Mr. Micheldene.'

Roger peered at Castlemaine. 'Is that all he told you?'

'Look at me, sir. Study my countenance. Do I seem to
be holding anything back?'

'No. Very well. Good-night to you.'

Roger went to a bar opposite the college entrance and
ordered a large whisky and water with no ice.

The barman repeated the order and added inexplic-
ably: 'And a double self-communion. Coming up.'

It was unjust, Roger considered, that he should have got
virtually no information out of Castlemaine after subjecting
him to a kind of pressure that, to some judges, might
savour a little of blackmail. But more important was the
difficulty of deciding what to do next. Macher and Helene
were probably not in Harlem or Central Park or Wall
Street, but that still left a lot of Manhattan to search from
scratch. Then Roger realised that he knew of one place to
look. The chances of its being the right place were perhaps
not high, but he had no other lead at all. There was one
trifling inconvenience to be endured first.

Twenty minutes later he was listening to the thrilling
ecclesiastical chimes that resulted from pressing the bell-
button at Strode Atkins's front door. The master of the
house, wearing a mustard-coloured velvet smoking jacket
with lilac piping, answered the summons in person. 'Hi,
Mitch,' he said as if glad to see Roger. 'Come right on in.'

In the living-room, Roger soon picked Mollie out from

among the terra-cotta figurines and witch-doctor masks. 'What brings you here?' she asked him.

'I was just passing.'

'Going to get you a brandy Alexander,' Atkins said. 'Good for keeping the cold out. I know it hasn't been cold yet but it's best to be on the safe side. The weather can turn awfully sharply in this part of the State. Shan't keep you a minute. You'll entertain Mollie, won't you?'

When Atkins had gone out to the kitchen, Mollie said neutrally: 'I didn't really expect to see you again much. What do you want?'

Roger decided some slight preamble was called for. 'Look, if I said anything uncalled-for the other evening I want to say I'm sorry.'

'But if you only said called-for things then you don't want to say you're sorry, is that right?'

'I was frightfully tight and I don't remember much about it, I'm afraid.'

'Bully for you. Oh, hell. What do you want, Roger?'

'This is very urgent and complicated or I wouldn't dream of asking you. I want the key of your flat in New York.'

She looked away. 'Oh.'

After a long pause, he said: 'There isn't much—'

'Oh, we've plenty of time.' There was a crash and a curse from the kitchen. 'See what I mean?...I feel I should do what I can to protect my fellow-women but you know it's impossible for me to say no, you son of a bitch. How would I look to myself? All right, I'll give it to you when you leave, which I imagine will be soon. The address is on the tag. Oh, what a bastard you are.'

'I know.' Roger tried to look ashamed. 'But it's too late to change.'

There was some more silence until Atkins came out of the kitchen and handed Roger a glass of thick tan-coloured stuff. 'More than a food,' Atkins said : 'a drink.' Then he laughed.

As he held up his glass to them Roger was congratulating himself on the sudden flash of uncanny insight which had led to him to disguise his motive for wanting the key. To have perceived this paradox, that they would abet disloyalty to themselves but might shrink from helping to make things awkward for one of their own sex, one who in this case was in some sense a rival—what was this but to understand women?

CHAPTER XV

Roger listened hard at the door of the flat. Nothing. There was no light from under the door either, but perhaps it fitted unusually well. Not that the condition of the lobby downstairs or of the lift made this likely. Anyway. At Pennsylvania Station he had dallied with the thought of a reconnoitring telephone call, but even if he had rung off instantly on hearing Macher's or Helene's voice (an unlikely provision in his present mood) some surprise-value would have been lost. And in any case they would surely have let the thing ring. This second consideration settled his last doubts about having omitted to ask Mollie not to tell Strode what was going on. Confident intuition that the state of the Atkinses' marriage ruled out this chance was no substitute for the knowledge that Strode, even if he got to the stage of being baulked on the telephone, was not the man to drive to New York simply in the hope of preventing or alleviating an ugly scene. Roger listened again. Still nothing. Out or asleep. He turned the key and entered silently.

The first thing was a slight smell of dust and soot. The furniture was humped against the light from the street. However gently he moved the floor gave and creaked under his feet like a disintegrating raft. Then he made a loud remark and clawed at the walls until a battered copper chandelier came to life—if the guilty couple were here he would be able to insist on having a word or so with them before they left or were rendered unconscious or whatever was in store for them. He explored. There was a

single bedroom that nobody was using and a bathroom and
a kitchen and a double bedroom with a very expensive bed
in it that somebody was or had recently been using : two
people, in fact, to judge by the bathroom shelf. But were
they the right two people?

Roger tried to remember if he had ever seen Helene
wearing any of the articles—earrings, a striped cotton
shirt, a blue suede skirt—that seemed to belong to a current female occupant, but without success. Normally he
had less than no time for that kind of accomplishment,
deeming it best confined to homosexuals, but it would
undoubtedly have come in handy now. He rubbed his
podgy nose. It might be awkward to find himself confront-
ing other acquaintances of Strode's : a Milwaukee wrestler
and his wife, a New York State Legislator and a hat-check
girl. He left the bedroom and wandered about pettishly.
Then, behind the bathroom door, he found something he
was fairly confident of having seen in the last week or so,
a housecoat affair with stripes of pale blue and white.
Inspiration sent him to the label. It said *lundqvist modes
københavn.* Being sure made a surprising difference. Roger
discovered he was short of breath.

Well, what now? Eleven-forty. They should be back
soon. But then people, at no time remarkable for behaving
as they should, seemed in the last week to have given up all
pretence of doing so. Macher and Helene might not be
back till two-forty. Or four-forty. Roger was pretty confident that he himself, faced with the prospect of a whole
night with Helene, would have had her back from dinner
by eight-forty. Or six-forty. But Macher was different. It
was entirely conceivable that he would turn out to be
interested in sleeping with Helene only in the literal sense,
would shake his head and do his laugh on finding that
Roger supposed otherwise. Conceivable but unlikely.

Roger decided he would very much prefer not to hang

round this flat for two or three hours in his present state. Perhaps he could modify his present state. He ransacked the place for drink. There was a little whisky, about a treble, which he drank without looking at it. There was a slightly larger quantity of dry vermouth which he drank after looking cursorily at it. There was about a third of a bottle of Californian rosé which he drank after very carefully examining it. He looked at his watch. Eleven-fifty.

At one stage in his searches he had noticed food without its arousing any response in him. Had he dined? To set about eliciting this information from himself at any other time could only have betokened extensive brain-damage. No, he had not dined. He went back to the kitchen and put down a piece of bread and a glass of milk. The bread was like friable cardboard and the milk like liquid cardboard. Eleven fifty-three.

He examined the front door of the flat for any bolt or other device that could stop someone with a key from entering. There was none. He made sure he had Mollie's key with him and went out. After standing in the street for a few minutes he walked along to an intersection, saw a taxi and hailed it.

'Is there jazz taking place in this city tonight?'

'Yeah, I reckon so. Yeah, you could say that.'

'Take me to where it's being played.'

He was driven to Broadway at great speed and set down in front of what they called in their language a marquee. At the entrance two Negro women behind a window told him that that would be one dollar eighty. He explained that he only wanted to see if some friends of his were inside and had not come to listen to the music. They said that he was very welcome to do just as he pleased and that would be one dollar eighty. He told them that that was extortion and he was going in and be damned to them. Two of the biggest and most muscular men he had ever seen in his life, both Negroes, came over and stood and looked at him. He handed over a dollar eighty and moved towards the strange and dreadful noises coming from the interior of the establishment. These grew sharply in volume as he entered the main auditorium and seemed to acquire a faint tactile quality, like a continuous shock-wave.

Several hundred people of various colours were present, all standing or sitting very close to one another. It was also very dark. Roger soon divined that it was going to be most difficult to find out whether Macher and Helene were here or even to exercise the divine gift of free will in any particular. But one such effort in that direction must certainly be made. He began shoving and twisting his way towards the bar that ran down the left-hand side of the room. By the time he got to it the noises had stopped, there had been applause, and a tiny Negro with a squeaky voice had launched into a long hugely amplified harangue of evident introductory intent. Roger ordered three large whiskies, poured them all into one glass, added water and took a hefty initial pull. A lanky Negro in an olive-green suit of which all three jacket-buttons were fastened was watching this carefully. He turned his sunglasses on Roger (what could he still see?), gave a cordial smile and said:

'Man, ya beez lan wah yam reez a heez woo nap lah cam a nam.'

'I beg your pardon?'

A shorter but blacker Negro on Roger's other side turned his head. This man wore a narrow-shouldered charcoal-grey suit which made him look very sedate, of a higher order of society altogether than the groups of arguing white men at the nearby tables. He said with an air of indulgent explanation:

'Wa hang heez a beez mah gat sam reez a ran moo pah yah dan, man.'

'I fear I fail to understand you.'

This occasioned no surprise or resentment. The two men exchanged a few remarks across Roger, seeming finally to arrive at a shared theory about him that in no way imperilled his self-esteem. Both nodded courteously at him and turned their attention to the stage.

In the intervals of looking about, rather perfunctorily, for Macher and Helene, Roger too found himself noticing events. After great hardship he reached the lavatory, which was of a size that might have been expected aboard a rather cramped day-excursion steamer. Slogans informed him that Zoot was something else, that Bird lived and that CCNY ate it. On his return Roger found that yet another Negro, whose moustache stretched from cheekbone to cheekbone, was talking, doing more introductions. But this one was a funny one. Roger could easily tell that from the way the people kept laughing at what he said. They applauded and shouted enthusiastically in addition when he told them he wanted to thank them and added: 'Well look, here's Daz MacSkibbins Vouts O'Rooney and his trumpet.' O'Rooney had a small goatee beard and wore sunglasses and carried an instrument that someone, in a fit of rage no doubt, had bent in the middle. The man O'Rooney was of Negro race. Roger stared apathetically at him, finishing his drink. Attempts to buy something to take away met a polite refusal, and the idea of going in search of a liquor-store was fatiguing, so he decided on another three-in-one for the road. A certain John Colvoutie and three other persons of Afro-American descent had been presented to the audience before Roger abandoned whatever had been his project here and struggled to the exit. He was only just in time. The noises had begun again, and a fearfully prolonged wavering squeal— O'Rooney? Colvoutie?—hung in the air as he departed.

Outside, he again stood in one place for a time. It was

twelve-fifty. Something that Ernst had said penetrated slowly to him. When a taxi came he said to its driver:

'I want to go where there's some authentic jazz. Could you find it for me?'

'Let's see, there's a West Coast outfit or so, and there's bossa nova, and the M.J.Q. are in town, and there's that stuff at Jimmy Ryan's, or maybe you'd prefer Eddie—'

'I want authentic jazz. Is there any?'

'Oh, now I get it, you want authentic jazz.'

'Take me to where it's being played.'

There was no marquee or anything like that this time, and all the performers and most of the patrons were white, and there was much more room, and a lot of people were dancing, but the noises were just the same. A policeman at the entrance gave Roger a postcard-sized card which said: *We want you to have a good time—but—we must insist on proper behaviour,* and went on to mention some of the things Roger might do which would result in his immediate ejection. He found a small bar at which, under the eye of a policeman, he ordered three large whiskies. He was given a glass jug holding about two pints of beer for which he paid. At the edge of the dance-floor he looked for a chair to sit on and eventually came to one of several which had its back tipped forward against a table. He untipped it and sat down, but a policeman explained that its earlier tipped position meant that it was reserved for somebody else and he must not sit there. After a time he noticed some chairs stacked against a wall. Watched by two policemen, he unstacked one and sat on it. When his beer was finished he toured the floor in search of Macher and Helene, muttering to himself. They were not there. A long queue at the bar prevented his getting more beer there, so he went to a table where two small men were sitting with two small women and helped himself from their jug. He moved his mouth about and glared fiercely at them as he did so and none of the four spoke or moved. But, although the theft of beer was not mentioned on the card he had been given, what he had done resulted in his immediate ejection. Three policemen were concerned in this. Their insistence that he should not try to re-enter the place was unmistakable, but they made no attempt to injure him.

From inside the taxi everything looked foreign. A number of typical American citizens stood in a leather-jacketed huddle on a street corner, idly watching a white-clad man in a shop throwing what might have been some foodstuff into the air and catching it again. There were other shops that offered to sell him things he would not be needing, notably Persian carpets. Several times Roger caught sight of signs and such in the Italian language. Then the taxi rushed past a number of identical box-like redbrick buildings—the secret police barracks, no doubt, or the various departments of the propaganda ministry.

It was dark in the street when he left the taxi. There was nobody about, though he could hear some sort of concerted shouting in the distance. Beside the main steps of the apartment building he could have sworn he saw a number of dustbins. The lid of each was secured by a chain. Roger pondered about this for some time. It must be possible to remove the lids temporarily, otherwise the contents of the bins could not be emptied out, nor, if you thought your way back far enough, put there in the first place. He grasped the railing by the steps and watched the bins and their lids. Then the solution struck him: the chains were to prevent people from taking off the lids and running away with them and selling them. How much would a dustbin-lid change hands at? What sort of culture was it, he asked himself, that took precautions against dustbin-lid-thieves while some people, *other* people, were watching colour TV and going to Vermont on shooting trips? Answering his own question put him to no trouble whatever. He had known it all along.

He decided the intellectual difficulties raised by the lift were worse than the physical ones raised by the stairs. Here and there he noticed empty niches that perhaps had once contained images of Our Lady. At the door of the flat he went through the same routine as before with the same eventual result: there was nobody there. This struck him immediately as very unjust. The three bottles he had emptied earlier proved on inspection to be still empty. He felt at something of a loose end. Strolling from room to room on burnt and holed fitted carpeting that had once been pearl grey, he just about noticed a gramophone with an almost incredible number of heat- and spirit-rings on its lid, a one-armed New England rocking-chair, a sofa of some slight interest as an anti-personnel device (wherever all this had come from it had not been from Miranda), a stained pitch-pine shield on which was mounted the stuffed head and neck of a dachshund. Beneath this a copper strip said: Mitzi * 1946-1953. Had Strode been devoted to this animal or had he shot it? Probably both.

Roger turned next to the bookshelves, which had some time ago been painted so as faintly to recall the gorgonzola type of marble. On them there stood or leaned several dozen proof copies and a couple of hundred bound books, all evidently novels, all in bright and effective eye-repelling jackets, all giving off a tang of mingled immediacy and obsoleteness. He regarded them with a half-hearted distaste which few save the initiated would have thought appropriate to one professionally concerned in putting living literature into the hands of the many, or at any rate of the relatively numerous. An inside wrapper, swung away from the binding into a position probably destined to remain frozen for ever, carried several citations to the effect that the book in question extended the tradition set going by

Jane Austen and kept going by Henry James. Roger had never heard of its title or author. He yawned in particular and in general: he felt, as always, that what he could not do with was a good read.

The desk, surmounted by a beaten-up typewriter and carrying evidence of many years of devoted cigarette-smoking, looked more promising. There was some apparently recent correspondence. Roger picked up a sheet hastily torn from a pad that bore a few ill-written lines in green ink. Without formality the writer announced that he had recently arrived in the United States from the United Kingdom, wanted assistance in finding a publisher for a book of his about South America, considered chiefly from educational and other social points of view, and would be sending the typescript along 'in due course'. He would be writing again 'before very long' and signed himself 'L. S. Caton'. The other letters were of even less interest.

Roger started on the drawers of the desk. None was locked and all were at least half full of typescripts in card-board folders. In general they seemed far less recent than the correspondence and went one stage further than the novels on the shelves in having no past as well as no present or future. This prenatal graveyard of the written word was a healthy and cheering sight but it offered the puzzling suggestion that at one time Atkins must have done some work of a sort. How could that have come about? Roger cheered up a little at the thought that he was never going to have the chance of finding out that or anything else to do with Strode Atkins.

This brought on the arrival in Roger's head of a fully formed notion, the first for some minutes. It was not un-likely that one of these drawers was the abode of *Perne in a Gyre*, the sole literary utterance of that talentless nuclear-disarmer brother-in-law of his who believed all British pub-lishers to be leagued against him in an imperialist and unnecessary conspiracy. And the recovery of this typescript must substantially improve his standing with Pamela. 'Managed to get my hands on it somehow. Took a bit of doing, but...' —'Oh, Roger, you didn't. How marvellous.'

After a drink of water he began a systematic search of the desk drawers. In time he came to one next to the bottom which resisted his efforts to pull it out. It had no handle and was unusually full, so much so that the top layer of stuff kept catching against the inside of the frame. But it was not locked and a few Joe-like tugs did the trick. Half-way down, between two tattered folders, he came upon a small oddly-sized book bound in marbled paper on boards. He picked it up clumsily and an oblong card fluttered out from between the pages. The brownish handwriting on it was hard to read. It seemed to say :

Lord H	*1 lash*
Wm	*2 lashes*
Watts	*3 lashes*
Gabriel	*10 lashes*
Algernon	*50 lashes*

Three minutes later Roger was certain that, while the contents of the notebook might not be the best of Swinburne, or the most creditable of Swinburne, or even the most rewardingly discreditable of Swinburne, they were Swinburne. As such they demanded to be removed from American hands. Their other demands could be gone into in due course. He had all the time in the world to fill the drawer again and close it, to put the notebook away in one of the special inner pockets of his jacket, before the expected taxi arrived below the window. He had the lights off within a couple of seconds and had been standing in position, his hand on the switch, for nearly a minute when he heard the lift gates.

CHAPTER XVI

THE EFFECT WAS all he could have hoped for. When he put the light on Helene cried out and her body jerked twice. Even Macher took a second or two to restore his eyes and mouth to normal. Then he grinned and said:

'This is very clever of you, Mr. Micheldene. Obviously you have an excellent memory for some things. I never thought you were listening when Strode told me I could use this place.'

'Oh, I do a fair amount of listening,' Roger said in his quietest voice. In the last few hours he had wondered from time to time what he was going to do if and when his moment came. Now he knew, at least as regards the opening moves. But there was no rush. 'I think perhaps I've managed to work out what my role in your life is. Fortunately it's one that can be adequately defined in terms of practical demonstration, so there's no need for me to bother with words.' He advanced on Macher, who stood his ground. Roger went on: 'Let's see how you get on when it comes to using violence in defence of someone you like or love.'

He was still not within range when Helene strode forward. Her thin lips were thinner than usual. 'Let's get one thing straight,' she said in level, decided tones. 'If anybody hits anybody, if anybody so much as touches anybody I go right out that door and I never speak to either of you again ever. Is that clear? Roger, is that clear?'

He found it hard to answer. To explain how he felt about hitting Macher and not hitting Macher seemed to him of unique importance, but however carefully he put it he was doubtful whether she would understand, or even try to. He shook his head slowly and blinked. 'But I wasn't going to really . . . hurt him,' he pointed out. 'Only fists. No foot or knee or anything like that. Nothing below the belt, honestly. No rough stuff at all.'

'If you lay a finger on him you're through. I mean it.'

Roger still felt uneloquent. After a moment he gave a loud sneering snuffle. 'How does it feel,' he asked Macher, 'to have your lady-love pleading for your life? A real man wouldn't be able to—'

'Just fine. She's much more persuasive than I'd know how. And I'm not a real man. I'm a very unreal man. You're the real man around here.'

'You're a child, not a man,' Roger shouted. 'Men have to learn to play by the rules, damn it, but not you. Oh no. You want something so you just take it. Don't know what it means to earn the right to something. Just come crashing in and . . . Like all your bloody countrymen. It'd be funny if it weren't so terrifying. You freckled fool.'

'Do you mind if I sit down?' Macher asked, doing so circumspectly on the edge of the sofa. 'Of course, I realise this is rather unfair on you, not being allowed to hit me. I suppose one does—'

'Think yourself bloody lucky you're being protected. I'd have reduced you to pulp in two minutes. Less than that. Ten seconds. That's the trouble, you're pulp already. One tap would lay you out. You'd be grovelling and pleading and begging me not to—'

'It certainly would and I certainly would,' Macher said with conviction. 'I haven't been hit since I was twelve years old. I didn't like it then and nothing's happened meanwhile to change the way I feel about it.'

'You're just a miserable smooth-talking posturing little coward.'

'A coward, certainly. But what you don't seem to understand, Mr. Micheldene, is that this is all right with me. It
gives me a tremendous advantage over you. I'm not only
a coward, I'm also a liar and a thief and I value worldly
success too much—I'm not as spiritual as you—and I have
other defects we needn't go into right now. But the point is
I know all this and I *don't mind*. Now if you were more
adaptable you'd find out something about me I did mind
and you'd work on that. It's getting kind of late in the day,
though, for any such innovations on your part, isn't it?'

'Macher, before this thing of yours gets any worse I'd
seriously advise you to put your pride in your pocket and
go and see somebody really good.'

'Sorry—that's another rubber arrow. If being the way I
am includes a neurosis of some sort, as it probably does,
then let it. In any event—sticks and stones may break my
bones, only we're agreed sticks and stones are out, and
words will never hurt me, no words you're likely to think
of uttering anyhow, so what are you going to do?'

'Going to do?'

'Precisely so. What are you going to do? What's your
personal policy for the next few hours, more particularly
for the next one?'

Helene had been standing nowhere in particular nearby,
staring angrily at Roger all the time. Now she joined in:
'Why don't you just go away, Roger? There's nothing for
you to do here. You're not going to have a fight and we've
nothing to say to you and you've nothing to say to us. So
go home.'

'I've plenty to say to you, young woman, make no
mistake about that, and you're going to—'

'Oh, *God*.' Helene put her hands over her face. 'I don't
want to hear. If only you knew how much I don't want to
hear. I just want to go to bed.'

'Yes, I'm sure of that.'

She snatched her hands away from her face. 'Get out of my sight, you fat slob. How I ever let you touch me I can't—'

'No, Helene,' Macher interrupted, 'not like that. That's the way he likes it. We do it differently. Look, let me show you.' He put his tongue out at Roger and chanted : 'The British are coming, the British are coming. Shoot the British, shoot the British. Roger came bottom of the class —yah-yah de yah-yah, yah-yah de yah-yah.' He put his thumbs on his ears and waggled his fingers. 'Roger can't write, Roger can't figure, wow wow wow, wow wow wow.'

'Fellow's...fellow's absolutely... How you could ever have...with a fellow... Marry a fine chap like Ernst and then...with a fellow...'

'Leave Ernst out of this, do you mind?' Helene said, her mouth sticking out.

At this verbal cue Roger's mind came a little way out of its trough. 'Well, you certainly managed to leave him out, didn't you? Nice chap like that, I don't understand how you could do it. Practically out of his mind with worry, do you realise that? I saw him this evening, spent a long time with him as a matter of fact, and the poor devil was practically out of his mind. With worry. How you could have—'

'Nonsense, he knows I'll be back. I set everything up so that he needn't—'

'To your way of thinking you may have *set* everything *up* to perfection, but I know different. In those far-off days when you were coming away with me this weekend, before you changed your mind in your little feminine way and decided you preferred this frightful young shit... What happened to the idea that you were going to visit your aunt in Cincinnati? Arthur thought you were, but Ernst had no illusions about—'

'I just found I couldn't lie to him.' For the first time

Helene's manner showed lack of confidence. 'I was ready
to but I found I couldn't. But he knows I'll be back.'

A keening, almost elegiac note entered Roger's voice.
'Why did you do it, darling? Oh, why did you have to do
it? Why did you have to be so angry with me?' His voice
steadied. 'You were angry with me, weren't you?'

'I certainly was. But it doesn't matter now.'

Roger's mind's eye was momentarily filled with an image
of Saturday night. 'You had no reason to be. Nothing
happened. All she did was bite me. Here, you can look if
you want.'

'I don't want to look. Look at what?—What's this
about, Irving, do you know?'

Macher had been doing his laugh, more slowly and
quietly than usual. 'I'm afraid I do, a little. He made a
play for Suzanne on that island Saturday night and she bit
him and then he didn't make a play for her any more.—
I'm sorry about that, by the way. I guess I was partly
responsible. Not for the bite: that was Suzanne's idea and
it rather shocked me. Very crude. I'd hoped she'd have had
more imagination. She's surprisingly immature in some
ways. Oh, she's a nice girl but she's a little too sold on my
ideas. Not enough independence of judgment. Have to
give her time.'

'How do you come into this?' Helene asked Macher.

'Suzanne and I decided it might be fun to see how Mr.
Micheldene would react if he got the impression she
might be available. I suppose it occurred to me first. But
then I had a special interest in it. I already knew I had
some chance of making you—I didn't know how good a
chance. It was easy enough to see our English friend was
very interested in you. I wanted to find out how exclusive
this interest was. I got the answer. Not very.'

Helene nodded tiredly.

'You mean you didn't know anything about this Suzanne business?' Roger asked.

She shook her head. 'How could I?'

'I thought you saw us. I thought I saw someone watching us wearing that white dress of yours.'

'Oh, I spy on necking couples, do I?'

'No, I didn't mean—'

'Your anxiety was unnecessary. I wasn't wearing that dress that evening.'

'You weren't? Well, what made you so angry with me? What had I done?'

'You'd behaved like you.'

'In what way?'

'Do you really want to know?'

'If you folks will excuse me,' Macher said, 'I guess I'll go take a bath. Or maybe a shower. I'll see how I feel when I get there.'

When he had gone, Helene said: 'All right then, Roger. Since you ask me. It was wrong of me ever to say I'd come away with you. But you'd just been nice the way you sometimes are, without meaning to be, not trying to get something out of me. Then I thought too, if I could do this it would stop me feeling bad about you for quite a while, so—'

'Feeling bad about me? Why do you feel bad about me? How?'

'When I go to bed with you I feel less sorry for you, you bug me less, I stop feeling responsible for you, and when you're awful I can just be bored with you and mad at you in the same way I might at anyone else, it doesn't get me all tensed up and involved, so when you insisted on trying to call Maynard Parrish that afternoon when you could have been with me a little longer I was just disappointed, I wasn't all . . . disturbed and . . .'

'Is that the only reason you've gone to bed with me, because you feel...? Haven't you enjoyed it, ever?'

'You wouldn't know, would you? It's all for you, all that, isn't it? You think of it and you do it. Like a lot of men. You know, the first few years I slept with people I thought it was all a thing they did to you. If you happened to enjoy it and you showed it that was all right, that was fine because it told them how good they were, but you didn't have to enjoy it too much because you weren't there for that. Then I met someone who looked at me sometimes when he was making love to me, didn't keep his eyes shut all the time the way the rest of them did. He knew I was there. From start to finish. So I married him.'

Roger saw with astonishment that a bottle of whisky had appeared on a nearby shelf. Macher and Helene must have brought it back with them, he concluded. He opened it and took two hefty swigs. 'You don't like me at all,' he said, coughing. 'Do you?'

'It isn't that. You don't like me.'

'Helene, I love you. I love you and I want to marry you.'

'Maybe you do, but you don't like me. You know when I decided I wasn't coming away with you? Saturday night when I was driving you into town to see your priest. The way you talked to me then.'

'But I was drunk then. I didn't know what I was saying. What did I say? I bet you can't remember either. Come on, what did I say?'

'I don't know, I wasn't listening, I was doing my best not to notice what you said. But I couldn't not notice the way you were saying it. You were saying it the way someone talks when he doesn't like the person he's talking to. When I realised that it was much worse than any time you've been awful.'

'If I mean as little as that to you,' Roger said, taking

another swig and putting the bottle back on the shelf, 'why
did you ever say you'd even consider coming away with
me for good?'

'You've no idea how much this has worried me. I guess
I couldn't face telling you right there and then it was out of
the question. It was cowardly of me and I was a fool, I
knew I was a fool as soon as I told you I'd think about it.
I'm sorry, I shouldn't have said what I did.'

'It doesn't matter, I don't think I ever really believed it.'
Helene chewed hard at her thumbnail. 'Roger, will you
go now?'

'I do love you. I wish I was better at it.'

'Christ, will you go, please?'

Macher came back from the bathroom, carrying his
clothes, a towel wrapped round him. His manner was
different now. He said sharply to Roger: 'Why are you
still hanging around? What good are you doing? Helene,
why didn't you send him away? I have a lot of tolerance
ordinarily but by Jesus it's beginning to run out now. Go
away, Mr. Micheldene. Nobody wants you here. If you've
nowhere to go then go just the same.'

'Irving, listen to me a minute, will you?' Helene said.

'Sure, what is it?'

'You're not here so as to...as a way of showing you're
better than him, are you? You didn't bring me here to bug
him, did you?'

Macher smiled. He shifted his shoes from one hand to
the other and put his arm round Helene. 'No, it isn't why
I'm here. I think I'm better than he is anyhow. Maybe I'm
not really but I think I am. A view I could defend in argument any time you say. Any time but right now, that is.
No, I'm not here because of him. That's why you're here.
Oh, don't let's be neat about this—of course that's not the
only reason you're here, perhaps not even the main one. I
don't know. But we can leave that for the moment. What

we can't leave is the immediate breaking-off of Anglo-American relations.' With his arm still round Helene he turned to Roger. 'I told you to shove off. Shove off.'

'Please, Roger.'

'It's such a long way,' Roger said. 'Right up the other end of town. And it's so late.'

'You can get a cab.'

'I might not be able to. And it's so cold there, in my flat.'

'If it is it's the only place south of Maine that is,' Macher said. 'Go to bed in your clothes.'

'Can't I stay here, in that little room? I promise I'll keep out of your way in the morning. Please.'

'Please doesn't get you a bed under this roof. *Go... away.*'

'Oh, let him stay, Irving. What difference does it make?'

'You've got a point there.' He looked at Helene, at the ceiling, and at Roger. 'All right. But absolute silence must be maintained. No charging in with a fresh argument at five a.m. Agreed?'

'Yes,' Roger said. 'Thanks. Well...good-night.'

He was arranging his trousers over a chair by the bed when Macher came into the room. 'I understand you're going back to England in a few days,' he said, 'so I'd better tie up the loose ends now. I don't know whether you were going to make an offer for *Blinkie Heaven* but if you were don't bother. Strode Atkins tells me he can get me a better deal and I believe him. The other thing is this. I sometimes got the impression that you think some of the people in this country don't like you because you're British. That isn't so. We're out of the redcoat era now, even if you aren't. And we don't think in this way. We don't have group likes and dislikes. It isn't your nationality we don't like, it's you.'

CHAPTER XVII

'WELL, I'LL SAY good-bye, Roger,' Ernst said. 'Have a good trip, and don't attack that duty-free booze too hard, or you'll need another ocean voyage to recuperate. How long is it, six days?'

'Five,' Roger said. 'It was good of you to come along, Ernst, especially with your foot. How is it?'

'Oh, it's much easier now the cast's off. Just aches a bit if I stand on it too long. —I'll wait for you at the head of the gangway, darling. —Good-bye, Roger, old man. Keep safe.'

The two men shook hands and Ernst, leaning on a walking-stick, limped away along the deck of the liner among crowds of yelling or weeping children. There seemed to be a higher proportion of these among the passengers than ever before, which was saying a good deal. Helene said to Roger :

'The Derlangers don't look as if they'll make it.'

'No, Joe said on the telephone they might not. This is a busy week for him.'

'How was he? I haven't seen him since...'

'Since the party. He sounded very cheerful. Only one thing annoys him about his car, he said : he can't remember why he did it. He's going to reconstruct the crime with a five-dollar wreck from a scrap-yard and see what ideas come into his head.'

Helene laughed and Roger joined in. 'He's the most uncomplicated mixed-up man I've ever met,' she said. 'I'd better be going too, Roger. I don't want to keep Ernst standing there.'

'Yes. There's not much to say, is there? Except I'm sorry about everything.'

'So am I. But let's forget it.'

'Yes. How's Ernst been with you?'

'He doesn't punish me. It'll all be the same in a few weeks.'

'Thank you for not telling him I turned up that night.'

'It wouldn't have helped.'

'True enough. Well—can I come and see you when you're over the other side again?'

'We shan't be for some time. Ernst's been offered a two-year appointment in the linguistics department at Chicago —evidently it's a very good one—and it could lead to a permanent job there. He's going to accept and if we like it we're going to try to fix it to stay on. So it doesn't look as if you and I'll be seeing so much of each other in future. One thing, being over here next year will see to it there are no arguments about what nationality the baby is. Oh, I didn't tell you, did I? I was pretty sure I'd started it in Copenhagen but I wasn't certain until the other day. It'll be nice for Arthur to have a companion. I hope it's a girl.'

She looked at him, but he still said nothing.

'Well. If anyone had told me the other night I'd ever be sorry to see you go I'd have said they were crazy. But now it's happening I am. Good-bye, Roger.'

She kissed him on the cheek and left. A minute later he saw her and Ernst moving slowly down the gangway. Ernst was talking animatedly and Helene turned her head a couple of times to say things to him. Then they reached the customs shed and disappeared from sight.

Roger went below. The ship was full of passengers and fire-extinguishers. Three small men with beards and hats came out of the Scroll Room. Why was there no Scripture

Room? A uniformed man with a face that looked as if it had been liberally basted with hot gravy for the last hour approached with a lot of pieces of paper in his hand. 'Morning, Purser,' Roger said.

'And a very good morning indeed to you, Mr. Micheldene, sir. Very nice to have you aboard again.'

The Purser was an outstandingly horrible man. Seeing him some trips ago running the bingo session in the lounge, full of clickety-click and two walking sticks and one little duck on the water, Roger had started to feel sorry for him until he realised that the man enjoyed it. But it was good to be among one's own people again.

In his cabin Roger unpacked, had a wash and rang for the steward, to whom he gave a five-dollar sweetener and an order for a large whisky. While he waited for this to arrive he glanced briefly through Swinburne's notebook and locked it away in a drawer. It too was going back to where it belonged, roughly at any rate. Exactly where it would end up Roger had still not decided, though he had a premonition that it would be somewhere that paid well.

Noises and vibrations told him the ship was moving. He looked out of his porthole and saw the quay sliding slowly past. Then he wanted very much to cry and started to do so. This was unusual for him when sober and he tried to work out why he was doing it. It was obviously a lot to do with Helene, but he had said good-bye to her and to plenty of other girls in the past without even considering crying. What was so special?

Rage at the non-arrival of his whisky helped him to give up the problem. He dried his eyes on his green bandanna and took a pinch of Otterburn from his antelope-horn snuff box. Hitting his nose over the head with Macouba that night on the island had turned out to be the right policy: the double snuff-taker's nostril had retreated to two small pockets out of reach of the questing fingernail.

Another pinch, and he began to feel quite good. Soon he would be up to faring forth and starting to look over his female fellow-passengers. Something in him was less than enthusiastic about this course of action but he resolved to ignore it. Better a bastard than a bloody fool, he told it.

A knock came at the door. He went over his eyes quickly once more with the bandanna and had his back turned when the door opened and a voice said :

'It is. For Christ's sake, it is. Well, what do you know about that?'

Roger let Strode Atkins shake his hand but was beyond speech. Nor was this required of him for some time.

'I thought I saw you going aboard but I couldn't get to you. Then I had your name wrong but the Purser was a sweet guy and he helped me out. These boat-trips—I go over every year, you know—well, they can be a real drag but if you have the right kind of guy along they can be more fun. Really give you the chance to get to know some-one. Kind of life we live, that's pretty rare, eh, Mitch? —Come in. All right, put it down there, will you, and fetch me another of the same? Quick as you can. —You know, it makes me feel kind of funny, making this trip. Kind of romantic if that doesn't sound too silly. Returning to the land of my fathers, see? You knew I was of English des-cent, didn't you? Yes, my ancestors were English. Came to West Virginia in 1811. Now you'll probably say that was a pretty funny time to choose and I see your point, but... Hell, why go into it now? We've plenty of time.'